Praise for CHASING VERMEER

Very entertaining, this story also teaches something about art as it speeds towards its terrific climax.
INDEPENDENT

It can't be long before Chasing Vermeer by Blue Balliett is banned from schools, glorifying free thinking as it does, and recklessly encouraging children to go off-curriculum ... A classy production for cerebral children of 10-plus.
SUNDAY TELEGRAPH

This is a truly original interactive book, and one that will give plenty of entertainment to lovers of codes and puzzles.
ELEANOR UPDALE, JUNIOR EDUCATION

It's very well written with amazing chapter-by-chapter illustrations.
INDEPENDENT ON SUNDAY

Please read this in one sitting, for it brooks no interruption. A cult following might well develop.
BOOKSELLER

It is a compelling confection, beautifully produced, that will have robust readers hooked.
SCOTTISH SUNDAY HERALD

... a totally fascinating, daring, challenging, intriguing piece of writing ...
INIS

What an excellent concoction this is!
ACHUKA

From the Chicken House

Do you like intriguing, clever mysteries? How about one featuring ghosts in an amazing house? Actually, in this story it seems to be to be the house doing the haunting! Oh, and there's hidden treasure, a mysterious code …

Blue Balliett's brilliant new art puzzle will keep adults baffled until the end, but kids will understand exactly what's what!

Barry Cunningham
Publisher

2 Palmer Street, Frome, Somerset BA11 1DS

For my mother, Betsy,
who understands both carp
and dragons. B. B.

For my mother, Colleen. B. H.

First published in Great Britain in 2007 by
The Chicken House
2 Palmer Street
Frome, Somerset BA11 1DS
United Kingdom
www.doublecluck.com

Cover and interior design by Steve Wells
Printed in the UK by CPI Bookmarque, Croydon, CR0 4TD

1 3 5 7 9 10 8 6 4 2

British Library Cataloguing in Publication data available.

ISBN 978 1 905294 41 1

‘Fool that I am!’
said the Invisible Man,
striking the table smartly.
‘I’ve put the idea into
your head.’

– H. G. WELLS, *THE INVISIBLE MAN*

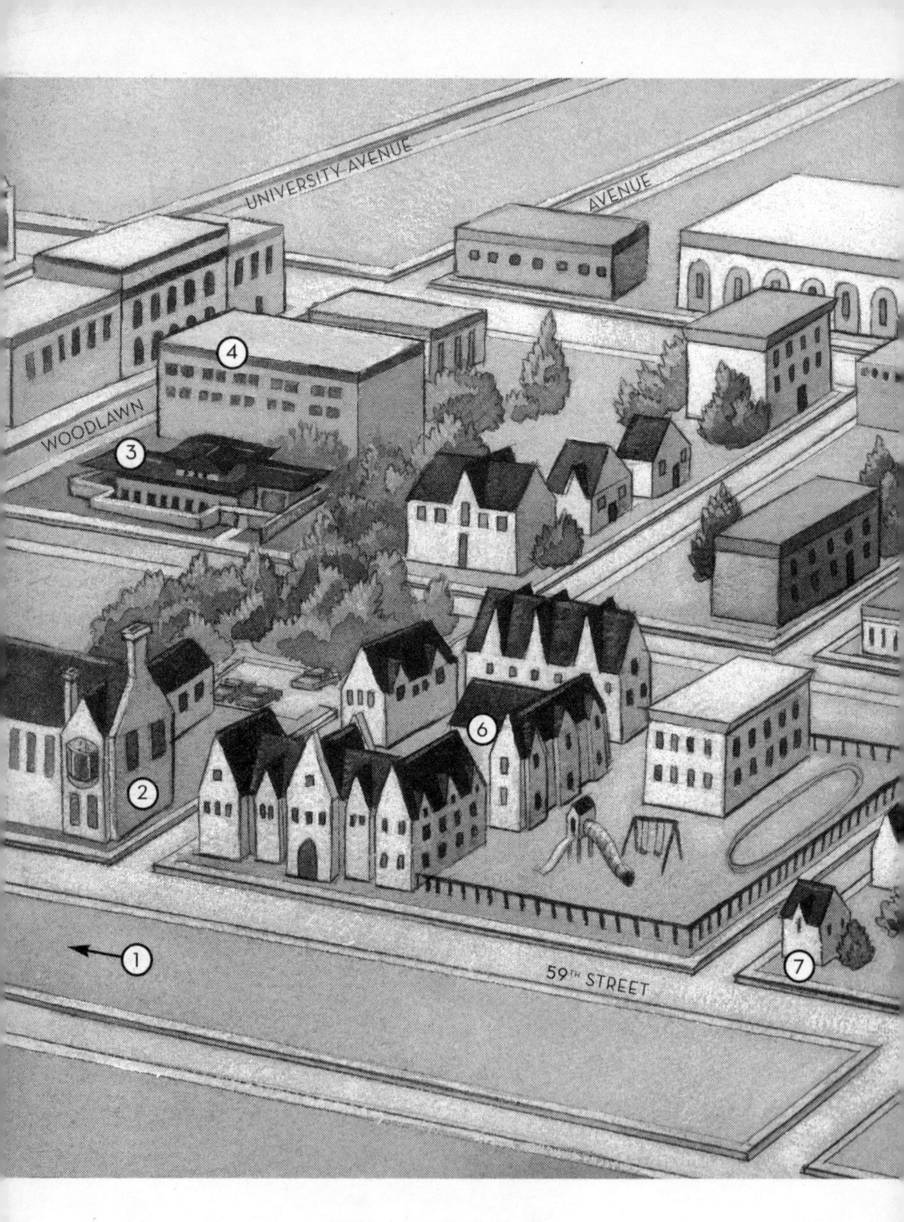

WRIGHT THREE MAP KEY

1	Hospital (ten-minute walk)	4	Tommy's apartment building
2	Delia Dell Hall	5	Medici Bakery
3	Robie House	6	University Middle School

7 Mrs Sharpe's house
8 Metro train entrance
9 Calder's house
10 Castigliones' tree house
11 Petra's house
12 Powell's Used Books
13 Japanese Garden (ten-minute walk)

ABOUT PENTOMINOES AND ABOUT WHAT YOU SEE

A set of pentominoes is a mathematical tool consisting of twelve pieces. Each piece is made up of five squares that share at least one side. Pentominoes are used by mathematicians around the world to explore ideas about geometry and numbers. The set looks like this:

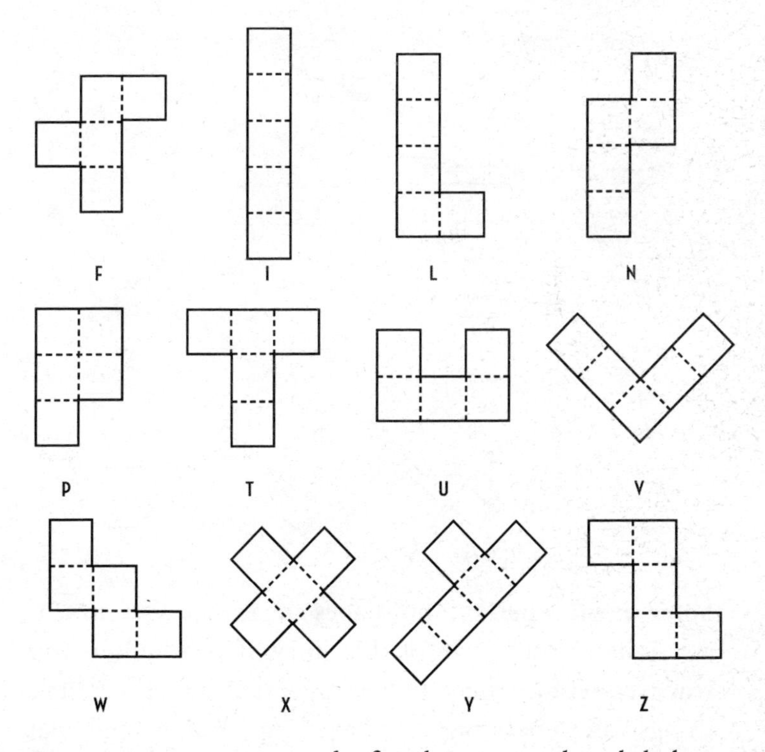

Pentominoes are named after letters in the alphabet,

although they don't all look exactly like their names. With a little practice, they can be put together into thousands of different rectangles of many sizes and shapes.

If the squares are changed to cubes, the same set of pentominoes can appear in three dimensions:

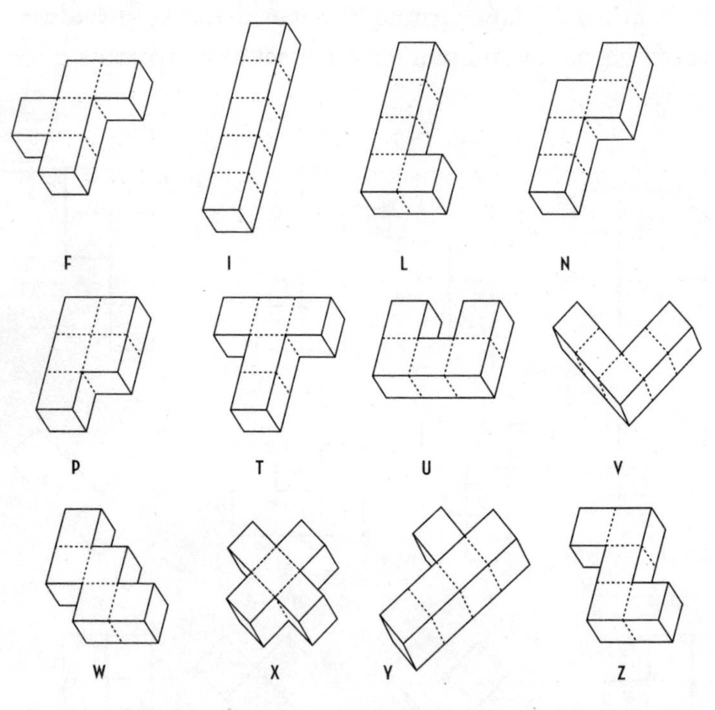

Some of these pentomino shapes are around you now, as are some of the pieces of this story. If you look as you read, you will see them. Don't forget that sometimes little things can appear big, and big things little – and that what you notice first isn't always what you're looking for.

ABOUT THE ARTWORK: A CHALLENGE TO THE READER

If you study Brett Helquist's chapter illustrations, you will discover many surprises. One of these appears in a pattern, and contains a creature that people all over the world enjoy. Some like it alive, and some prefer it dead. It changes form, and has appeared in stories and art for thousands of years.

Here's a hint: Both the creature and the pattern it appears in are hidden by nature, but if you look and count, you may catch what you see.

Chapter One

INVISIBLE

On the morning of 3 June, the mason climbed carefully to the highest level of the roof. He was alone and looked around happily: spring in Chicago, a day with no wind, and a world that was all new leaves. Smells of black earth and lilac mingled with children's voices from the school down the street, and he felt suddenly lucky.

I'm young and alive and almost invisible up here in the trees, he found himself thinking, and then shook his head at such a strange idea. Turning his attention back to the famous terracotta roof, he ran his hand along the chimney. A chunk of brick broke loose, rattling downward and landing with a distant *ping* on the terrace below.

At that moment he lost his footing. Startled, he flung his arms out for balance. Had he been standing on a loose tile? Was this an earthquake? He listened for car alarms, but the street below him was quiet. There was a second, longer shudder, and he

thought he saw the roof itself rippling towards him in quick, irregular lines. The building seemed to have come alive, twitching in the irritable way an animal does when it wants to get rid of a fly. The mason staggered to the left. Muttering 'What the—' he stumbled back to the right and sank to his knees.

His fall was sudden, a whirl of blue and branches and panic. He knew he would hit concrete. Copper gutters flashed by, and he landed heavily on the balcony outside the dining room. From where he lay, triangles in the stained-glass panels above his head flashed like sharp teeth. He struggled to breathe but felt as if a huge weight had landed on his chest; he was suffocating.

Invisible, his frightened mind whispered, you're invisible now. The house was empty, and he knew he was hidden from the street – he wondered if he would die before he was found. In the seconds before his vision melted into blackness, he thought he heard a high voice, the shrill command of a child, but he couldn't quite make out the words. Was it 'Stay away!' or 'Stay and play!'?

Chapter Two

MURDER IN THE CLASSROOM

Tommy Segovia looked out of his classroom window and chewed on a thumbnail that was already raw. He had been away for a year, and everything had changed – his home, his best friend, his teacher. Coming back to Chicago that June, he felt oddly like a ghost.

His old house on Harper Avenue, in the south-side community known as Hyde Park, had been painted a green that reminded him of unripe tomatoes. The bushes in front where he and his friend Calder Pillay had buried treasures – a rusty penknife found by the train tracks, a balloon filled with bottle caps, a cereal box of dead grasshoppers – had vanished. White flowers now puffed outwards in a stiff circle around the foundation. Tommy felt sorry for his house: it reminded him of a birthday cake that had fallen upside down.

Even Calder seemed different. Tommy always pictured him with his hair squashed in a straight-up position, fresh from sleep and no brushing, and at least one patch of dried food on his face. Calder's trainers were tied most mornings now, and he'd brushed his teeth. He still carried a set of pentominoes in his pocket, but they weren't the flat plastic ones that Tommy remembered. These were three-dimensional and made from small orange cubes. The pieces felt slippery and looked shiny, and you could almost see your reflection in the P. They made a different sound when Calder stirred them around in his pocket, more of a soft clatter than a sharp clack. Tommy liked the old sound better.

Calder lived across the street from Tommy's old house and had made a new friend on Harper Avenue while Tommy was gone. Her name was Petra Andalee. She had curly hair, thick glasses and small, quick hands. Her eyes made him think of an exotic monkey he had always admired at the Lincoln Park Zoo. He didn't think she'd like that idea, and he didn't know if he did either. They had accidentally collided yesterday on the stairs at school, and he noticed that she wasn't as bony as Calder, and she smelled like lemons.

They were all sixth graders now at the University School, and all twelve years old. Their teacher was new and young, and her name was Ms Isabel Hussey. She had long hair and lots of earrings, and yesterday she had worn pyjamas. Tommy didn't think she looked like a teacher at all, but to his amazement the class paid close attention to her. He tried, but there was so much to stare at and think about that it was hard to do anything else.

The classroom walls were covered with newspaper articles and odd quotes and paper footprints of all sizes. Appearing in every colour of the rainbow, the feet marched clockwise around the room, just under the ceiling, as if a kid were walking parallel to the floor. Calder explained to Tommy that each time you read a book, you wrote the title and author inside a tracing of your own foot and cut it out of card. Then Ms Hussey stuck it on the wall.

Books were not Tommy's thing, but looking at all those feet made him want to see his own up there too. He began wondering what he'd read during his year away that he could write down, but he couldn't remember even one title. How had Ms Hussey got the feet up there anyway? He pictured her balancing on the top of bookshelves and on the tray under the blackboard. No wonder she didn't wear skirts much.

One of the quotes Tommy first noticed was on the wall at the front of the room. It said, in black capitals on red paper:

ART IS THE MOST EFFECTIVE MODE OF COMMUNICATION THAT EXISTS.
— **John Dewey**, *Art as Experience*

Tommy knew John Dewey had started the University School at least a hundred years ago. He knew he was a smart guy, but he'd never heard Dewey was big on art. This quote seemed kind of silly. After all, art didn't actually say anything.

Another quote said:

ALL THERE IS TO THINKING ... IS SEEING SOMETHING NOTICE-ABLE WHICH MAKES YOU SEE SOMETHING YOU WEREN'T

NOTICING WHICH MAKES YOU SEE SOMETHING THAT ISN'T EVEN VISIBLE.

— **Norman Maclean,** *A River Runs Through It*

This one was hard to puzzle out but cool anyway, kind of like an optical illusion tucked into an illustration. Tommy loved looking at one particular page in every issue of the kids' magazine at his dentist's office, the trick page that had teapots or lizards or fish hidden in a line drawing.

He liked the idea of seeing things you can't really see.

Tommy knew from Calder that Ms Hussey and her class had spent most of last autumn investigating art. He was secretly glad he'd missed it, until something happened in December: Calder and this girl Petra stumbled on a big discovery. They found a stolen painting, a famous one by a guy named Vermeer. Newspapers wrote articles that praised Calder and Petra for being extraordinary detectives. This hurt for a couple of reasons: one, Tommy was a far better finder than his friend Calder, and two, before this they had done everything important together. If he hadn't been away, Tommy was sure it would have been Calder and him who recovered the painting, and recovered it in even less time. There was no doubt about it – he'd missed some major glory.

And then there was a horrible twist to the whole painting adventure: just over a year ago, Tommy's mum had met and married a man who had been the reason the three of them moved to New York last summer. He had seemed like a decent guy at first. That man, Tommy's stepfather, had played a part in the theft and then died of a heart attack before he could be arrested. Although Tommy had been told that no one blamed him or his mum for the crime, it was embarrassing that everyone in Hyde Park knew, and Tommy hated the idea that people might feel sorry for them.

They had planned to move back to Hyde Park during the summer holidays, but Tommy's mum had been offered her old job at the University Library, plus a small pay rise, if she started in early June. Because she was back at work, he was back in the classroom. So here he was with ten days left of the school year, and not a lot of time for making things better. He frowned and tried again to pay attention.

The class was now looking at architecture. The week before Tommy returned, they'd visited the Sears Tower and Frank Gehry's pavilion in Millennium Park. The class hadn't agreed yet on whether either structure was a piece of art. Ms Hussey asked lots of questions, like, Is a building a piece of art when you can't see all of it at the same time? Can a building be a piece of art on the outside but not on the inside and vice versa? She was usually calm and curious, but on this particular morning Tommy thought she'd gone a little crazy.

She was holding a newspaper article in her hand and hardly seemed to notice that the class was in front of her. Shaking her head slowly, as if whatever she was thinking about was impossible to believe, she said softly, 'Plunder in the name of salvation.' Then she repeated it, spitting out the syllables as if they were something disgusting that had got into her mouth. All rustling and chair-squeaking stopped.

She waved the article at arm's length. Her voice now dangerously cheerful, she added, 'Or perhaps a better term is murder.'

The class was silent.

Murder?

Chapter Three

LIFE & ART

Ms Hussey paced, her arms crossed and her plait flying out like a tail each time she changed direction. Today she wore red trainers, blue jeans and a long black scarf covered with a pattern of noodles. They were either noodles or short plumbing pipes.

She stopped and turned towards the blackboard. Picking up a fresh stick of chalk, she turned it over appreciatively at eye level. She then dropped it on the floor. The class gasped – she always got grumpy when someone else broke her chalk.

'There. If I pick up those pieces, will it still be the same piece of chalk? Will I have twice or three times as much? Will it still work the way I want it to?' No one said a word. Was this fancy maths she was talking about? And what did chalk have to do with plunder – or murder? Tommy had no idea.

'Let's try it.' Ms Hussey picked up a jagged chunk and turned towards the board. She wrote

LIFE & ART. The chalk made an ugly double line with each vertical stroke.

'Well?' Ms Hussey had her head on one side. 'I'm not really thinking about chalk, you know. I'm thinking about a house that some people think is a piece of art. I'm thinking about what happens when life and art don't mix well. I read about it in the *Chicago Tribune* this morning. Anyone know what I'm talking about?'

Calder's hand shot up. 'The Robie House?'

Ms Hussey nodded.

Tommy swivelled in his seat and studied the faces around him.

Calder went on, 'My parents said that people in the neighbourhood either love it or can't stand it.' His pentominoes were lying on his desk, and he now flipped over the L and completed a rectangle made from seven of the twelve pieces.

As Calder's fingers moved, the words life and art began to shift rapidly in his mind. If those seven letters were put in another order, life art became a trifle or a filter. He knew the word trifle meant something not too valuable or important, as his

Grandma Ranjana had sometimes used that word, and a filter could mean – well, something you looked through or poured stuff through. Life plus art equalled a trifle or a filter. Calder couldn't wait to tell Petra. She always understood when he discovered new ideas by rearranging the old ones.

'Duh.'

Ms Hussey frowned. 'Who said that? Denise? Tell us what you know about the house.'

Denise Schultz raised one eyebrow and studied her fingernails.

'Who built it, for instance?' Ms Hussey's tone was crisp.

Denise shrugged.

Ms Hussey held the article in front of her with both hands and read:

WRIGHT MASTERPIECE COMING DOWN

In a tragic piece of news for Hyde Park, the University of Chicago, owners of Frank Lloyd Wright's famous Robie House, announced today that the 1910 home will be donated, in sections, to four great museums around the world: the Museum of Modern Art in New York City, the Smithsonian in Washington, D.C., the Deutsches Museum in Munich, Germany and the Meji-mura Museum in Nagoya, Japan. The university cited an impossibly large number of structural repairs as the reason.

Many consider Wright to be the greatest architect of the twentieth century, and his Prairie Style jewel, the home built for Frederick C. Robie, to be a house that radically changed the domestic architecture of the United States.

The house was owned by three families before 1926, when it passed into the hands of the Chicago Theological Seminary. Affiliated with the University of Chicago and located just steps from the Robie House, the seminary used Wright's building for dormitory space, but allowed the structure to fall into serious disrepair. Wanting the land beneath it for new student housing, in 1941 the seminary announced that the house was going to be demolished.

It was Frank Lloyd Wright himself who came to the rescue. In an unprecedented move within the architectural community, he put together a committee of world-famous architects and art historians and declared the Robie House to be 'a source of worldwide architectural inspiration'. The seminary was shamed into keeping it.

The building limped on, looking worse and worse, until 1957, when the seminary announced that it was dangerous and would need to be torn down. They called a public meeting and showed completed plans for a large dormitory on that site.

Wright was then 90 years old and, brandishing his cane, returned to Hyde Park. He had recently completed plans for the Guggenheim Museum in New York City, and he was, by then, a national treasure himself. Describing the Robie House as 'one of the cornerstones of American architecture', and commenting that only the kitchen needed improvement, he persuaded William Zeckendorf, a developer, to buy the house from the seminary. Zeckendorf used it for office space and made plans to give it to the National Trust for Historic Preservation. In 1963, however, he changed his mind and deeded it to the University of Chicago, who remodelled much of the interior for departmental use.

John Stone, President of the university, said, 'It is only after extensive attempts to raise funds, both nationally and internationally, that we have made this painful decision. We have no alternative: the building, in its current state, is a hazard and needs many millions of dollars of renovation both inside and out. With great sadness and reluctance, we pass along a Wright treasure. The university cannot afford to keep it.'

The news has shocked architecture buffs around the world and left Hyde Park reeling. The Robie House was the only structure

Frank Lloyd Wright ever built, during a prolific career that spanned almost seventy years, that he fought to save, and he saved it not once but twice. Many believe that the house embodies his unique spirit and vision in a timeless form. It has come to occupy an almost mystical place in the annals of American architecture.

In a letter to the press, the university defends its decision as 'a bold move to provide many millions of people, around the world, with access to Wright's extraordinary work.'

A crew has already begun plans for the job. The actual dismantling of the house will begin on 21st June.

As one Hyde Park resident said, 'This breaks my heart. Hyde Park weeps.'

Ms Hussey looked up. 'I felt sick when I read this. A house like that needs light and air, and is one indivisible piece – the idea of carving up the structure and preserving chunks of it in *museums*!'

She said museums as if it was a dirty word, which was a little confusing. The class knew Ms Hussey loved to go to museums.

Tommy's hand was raised, but just barely. Should he tell the class that his new apartment was right next to one side of the Robie House? Would other kids think that was cool?

Ms Hussey was pacing now, her arms crossed, and didn't see Tommy's hand.

She went on, 'I know all of you have passed it many times – it's only three blocks away. The place looks modern now, but remember that it's been almost a century since Wright designed it. Things that seem normal to us were revolutionary then, like rooms that were no longer boxy, living space that flowed easily between inside and outside, front door hidden on the side of the house, deep cantilevered eaves, and an attached three-car garage.

'Many experts have said the same thing: there's a secret here. Wright thought in a geometrical way about lines, curves and surfaces, you have to see his work to understand, and even then it's hard to figure out what you're seeing.'

Ms Hussey stopped walking and turned towards the class, her mouth in a tight line. 'So: Art & Life.'

Another hand went up, and Tommy's sank down. Petra Andalee said, 'Can't the university just let the house sit there empty until the money comes in?'

Ms Hussey drew a quick breath as if she'd touched something hot. 'In an ideal world, yes. In the real world, no. The university probably can't afford to own a piece of property that they can't use, and if part of the house fell on someone walking by, the university would be held responsible.'

'Maybe we can visit the place and come up with ideas,' Calder suggested.

'I wish we could, but they haven't allowed visitors inside for over a year, and no family has lived there since 1926. This is deeply ironic, of course, since the house was built for children.'

Ms Hussey paused, twisting the end of her plait around one finger. The class waited, knowing this meant she was thinking about whether to share something.

'Actually,' she confided, 'I've always wondered about Mr Wright's focus on play space. At the time he was working on the Robie House, he had just left his wife and six children. And yet here he was, thinking creatively about what would make someone else's kids happy and safe. Maybe it was his way of asking the universe for forgiveness ...'

Tommy picked at a sticker on his desk, careful not to look up. Neither one of *his* dads had said sorry. When Tommy was a baby, his real dad had died in South America – he'd been arrested at a political demonstration and was never seen again. His stepfather had started out with a bunch of promises and then broken every one.

'Anyway,' Ms Hussey said, her voice businesslike again. 'It seems like a crime to destroy such a home, don't you think?'

'It doesn't look like a home to me,' one class member piped up.

'Really?' Ms Hussey said, looking pleased. 'Perhaps we have to figure out if the building is still a home, and whether a home can exist if it's empty. Or, beyond that, whether a home can also be a piece of art ...'

The class was quiet. Someone sighed. Ms Hussey looked around, then sighed also.

'OK – maybe it's too much to start an investigation so late in the year. But it's never too late to think. What could we do? Art-home or not, the Robie House has been a part of Hyde Park for as long as you, your parents, or maybe even your grandparents remember. It's just too horrible to think of it being pulled apart.'

Their teacher sat on the edge of a radiator. She had picked up a round, grey stone that lived on her desk, a rock with two bands of white that crossed neatly on either side. She called it her Lucky Stone, and the children knew when she picked it up that she was worried or upset. She held it now in both hands, her body a silhouette in the sunshine coming from the window behind her.

'But you said it was murder,' Calder blurted. 'You never give up! Why aren't you trying to

persuade us?' someone else said.

'I probably shouldn't have—' Ms Hussey broke off as an ambulance screamed by beneath the classroom window. Everyone listening would have been frightened by the coincidence if they had known who was inside: a mason was being rushed from the Robie House to the hospital, a man who had fallen quite a bit further that morning than the piece of chalk.

The bell rang.

Class was over, and Tommy stood up to go. He looked at Calder, three seats away. Calder glanced first at Petra and then back towards him. So that's the way it is, Tommy thought bitterly.

He hurried towards the door, passing Denise. She opened her eyes wide and then made them narrow again, as if to say she saw it all.

Tommy sped ahead, wanting to kick something.

Chapter Four

A FIND

At the end of the day, Tommy left school by himself. He didn't see either Calder or Petra on the way out. They lived three blocks east of the University School, and he now lived three blocks west.

He tried to tell himself that he didn't mind walking home alone. After all, he was living next to a famous house that was going to be torn apart. He could see it from his bedroom window, and if he watched he'd be witnessing a *killing*. Not a real one, of course, because a house was not a living thing. Ms Hussey didn't believe the experts who said they were saving the building by cutting it up; she thought their plan was selfish and cruel. Cruel ... Having a teacher who said something so extreme was pretty interesting.

As he headed home, Tommy looked carefully at Frank Lloyd Wright's building. It reminded him of an untidy stack of waffles, or perhaps a flat pyramid, or maybe a train carriage. Ms Hussey was right, the place was long and low and had lots of layers. Everything seemed pulled out in a tricky way, like one of those magic boxes where you slide a drawer out, close it, and a dollar bill disappears – only the drawers were still out. There were walls and roofs at about ten different levels, and hundreds of windows of all sizes. The stained glass in the windows was set in shifting patterns of triangles and parallelograms, and as Tommy walked slowly by, they seemed to wink and twinkle at him. He didn't remember noticing all the colours before – there were turquoises, blues, greens, purples. Wow – what a waste that this was all coming down.

The building was wrapped in heavy yellow tape. The tape said DO NOT ENTER over and over. Had that been there this morning? He didn't think so.

Once upstairs in his apartment, Tommy fed his goldfish. His mum, Zelda Segovia, wouldn't be home from her job at the library for another hour. Originally from England, she had silver hair that she kept squirrel-short and eyes that were two different colours, one chestnut and one blue. Tommy looked like his father, who was from Colombia. He and his mum had moved many times, and he was always careful to give his fish a window with a view. 'You're living next to an amazing building now, Goldman,' Tommy told his pet. The fish opened and closed his mouth, as if to say he understood. Goldman was a member of the family, and had been with Tommy for years.

As Tommy peered into Goldman's bowl, he looked through the water at the back wall of the Robie House. He was quite sure the house was empty, and he had a sudden idea. What if he just crept under that tape and poked around in the garden on the other side of the house? A wall separated it from the street, so he'd be more or less hidden. If he did some of his own digging, before anyone else from the class thought about coming over to investigate, he'd have news to share, and the kids would remember how gutsy he was. And what if he actually found a treasure?

After all, Tommy was a collector. His dad had been studying to become an archaeologist at the time he died, and his mum told him that finding must be in his blood. He'd been picking up and organizing 'street-gems', as his mum called them, ever since he could walk. He could spot four-leaf clovers without trying and had at least fifty of them pressed in a phone book. He had boxes filled with old lolly sticks, buttons, movie stubs and pieces of fire crackers. His prize collection, however, was fish, and he kept them on a special shelf: some were bright rubber or plastic, and others were postcards, carvings from Chinatown, black clay fish from Mexico, and presents people had brought back from trips. A wooden zebra fish lay next to a glass flounder with one silver eye. A coconut puffer-fish swelled above a tin trout. He even had a stuffed barracuda, complete with razor-sharp teeth, and a marzipan shark from Europe that had been too detailed to eat.

Tommy looked at the Robie House and whispered to Goldman, 'Wish me luck.' Then he zoomed out the door and down the stairs.

He waited until the sidewalk was empty, and slipped under the tape and into the garden. He crept along next to the wall in a half-crouch, his heart thudding.

Would he get in trouble if someone noticed him? He'd just tell a little lie, say he had spotted a quarter and gone after it. He knelt in the dirt and pulled out his digging tool, which had a fork on one end and a spoon on the other.

Ten minutes later, he'd found a red button, a lens from a pair of sunglasses, and an earring with one broken bead on it. Then his fork hit something larger.

He was down about twenty centimetres now. He dug with both hands, abandoning his tool. He'd uncovered a piece of carved stone about the size of a coat hook ... there! The clod of earth shot up with a little shower of pebbles. Tommy sat back on his heels, scraping off the packed dirt with his fingernails.

No – could it be? Jumping up, Tommy forgot to hide and leaped over the yellow tape with a whoop, almost knocking down an elderly woman with a cane.

'Not supposed to be in there, young man!' she

called after him, but he was too excited to stop. As he raced around the corner of the house, he glanced at the building, hoping no one else had seen him. The lines of leading in the first-floor windows looked suddenly like an empty fish net.

He thumped up the stairs, two at a time, to wash off his find.

Chapter Five

TALES FROM THE TRACKS

Petra and Calder walked home from school in near silence, as if Tommy's presence was all around them. Although they had often spent time together after school during the winter – puzzling over mysteries, eating or wandering around the campus – neither felt comfortable now.

Petra knew there'd be trouble from the first moment she saw Tommy again. That was two days ago, on 1st June, when Calder had arranged for them to meet in front of his house.

'Hey – you guys remember each other,' he'd said happily. Tommy had looked at the ground, and Petra at the sky.

Tommy was the smallest. From behind, his head had made Petra think of a black marble: it was amazingly round, and his hair was short and shiny. When he opened his mouth, she could see a chipped tooth that came to a point. His eyes were dark and looked like raisins stuck in gingerbread.

He kept his arms crossed on his chest, and talked as if Petra wasn't even there.

'Remember the time in third grade when we put liquid soap in the supply teacher's coffee?'

Calder had lit up, and punched Tommy in the arm.

'And remember the time we told the girl in the playground that we didn't speak English, and she spilled all those secrets?'

Calder had nodded and laughed, not seeming to notice Petra's discomfort.

She had left shortly after, mumbling something about homework. It was clear: Tommy didn't want some girl butting into his friendship with Calder. But this wasn't fair – Petra had never been a 'some girl' kind of person.

She had opened her front door that day to the faint smell of garbage and burned toast. Her younger sister galloped by with a shoe box on her head, driving their two younger brothers in front of her with a spatula. The dog rushed by with a toothbrush stuck to his back.

Petra had four brothers and sisters, and her house was a marvel of broken toys, runaway food and trainers of all sizes. Her father, Frank Andalee, was a physicist with family from North Africa and the Netherlands, and her mother, Norma Andalee, was a poet from the Middle East. Conversations happened at high volume and in a number of languages, and cheerful crisis was the norm: keys vanished, an important article had been used to line the cat litter tray, a mobile phone had fallen into the toilet. Nothing about the Andalee family was either simple or predictable.

Both Tommy and Calder were only children, and Petra envied them. Not having to cram down cookies when they were still too hot for fear of not getting one later, not having to help with tangled hair and sticky faces before school: it sounded so easy.

Hearing the door, Petra's mum had poked her head out of the kitchen. 'Can you pick up some milk and an onion for me? Now? Thanks, honey ...'

As Petra stepped back outside that afternoon,

she hoped Calder and Tommy had left. They had, and suddenly that was almost worse than seeing them again. Were they at Calder's? Was Calder telling Tommy how much he'd missed him?

Passing Powell's, the bookshop on the corner, Petra glanced into the give-away box that was always outside. Powell's couldn't keep all of the used books that people brought in, and many went into a cardboard carton to the left of the front door. Every Hyde Parker stopped and looked.

That day it was cookbooks, a dictionary, and a small, battered paperback, the kind that fits in a pocket. Petra picked it up. The cover was teal green and had a headless figure on it – a man standing calmly in a black suit, complete with white shirt and red tie. A bowler hat floated above the place where the face should have been. In between the hat and empty collar was a title.

'*The Invisible Man*,' Petra read aloud. She opened to page one. Someone had highlighted the words *an unheard-of piece of luck* with an orange marker. She flipped ahead, wondering whether to take the book home. She didn't particularly like reading things with underlining in them, but she didn't see any other markings.

At that moment a puff of warm air touched her cheek, as if to say, *Yes, take me*. She shrugged and tucked the book into the back pocket of her jeans.

With any luck, she thought unkindly, Tommy would become the Invisible Man.

⊞ ⊞ ⊞ But now, two days later, it was she who had become invisible – Calder was happy to see Tommy, and Tommy wasn't happy to see Petra. Even though she and Calder were finally alone now, things weren't the same. Lots had happened today at school, with all the news about the Robie House, but neither was talking.

They reached Petra's porch first, said goodbye, and she climbed the stairs quickly. Once inside, she went straight to her room.

Write, she told herself firmly, *write*. It always made things better. Think art. Think murder. Concentrate. All day her mind had felt dulled and kind of dented, like something had collided with it. Yeah, something like a kid with a round head, she thought to herself.

Petra's desk was lined up with the window sill. Gazing out, she opened her notebook and waited.

Harper Avenue was a narrow, crooked street that ran next to the tracks. Both Petra's and Calder's bedroom windows looked out on a landscape of horizontals and verticals peppered with gravel and leaves: metal tracks, the ties between them, the tall reach of tree trunks on both sides of the embankment. Petra loved the stories filed neatly into the flow of train windows – she had seen arguments in profile, mouths open with laughter or horror, noses squashed against glass. Depending on whether she held her eyes still or let them race with the carriages, she would see either a blurry sequence punctuated with bright threads of colour or a single glitter of a moment. She recorded these impressions in a section of her notebook called Tales from the Tracks, and planned to use them one day in a novel. The trains, it seemed to Petra, were always giving away valuable secrets.

Waiting here is a bit like taking a warm bath, Petra thought to herself, except it's looking through glass and not sitting in water, and you don't have to get wet. She sighed, knowing she had a weird way of putting ideas together in her mind. Metaphors and similes crackled across her brain like heat lightning in a summer sky. Sometimes she felt deep inside that she'd be respected one day for the things she wrote down, and she would push the thought away quickly. There was such a huge gap between being a real writer and being a kid who wanted to be one.

Although neither knew it at the time, Calder was also looking out his bedroom window. His parents wouldn't be home from work for another hour, and today he made himself a peanut butter and jelly sandwich and brought it upstairs while he waited. His Grandma Ranjana had died two years before, and ever since then the house was horribly quiet in the afternoons. If he was downstairs alone, he found himself noticing her empty rocking chair by the front window, and that made him both sad and spooked.

Like Petra and Tommy, Calder was an unusual mixture – his dad, Walter Pillay, was from India and planned city gardens, and his mum, Yvette Pillay, was Canadian and taught maths. His dad did most of the cooking and all of the gardening, and his mum did most of the talking and lots of intricate knitting. The family lived in a tidy, red house nestled in an experimental assortment of plants. Each had its own yellow tag in spring, and the Latin names bobbed and spun cheerfully until they disappeared beneath leaves.

As Petra waited that afternoon for a train story, Calder waited for a game of Blind Rectangles. He had made up the rules: first he dropped the set of pentomino pieces on his desk the moment a cargo train came into view, then he tried to form a rectangle while watching and counting the train carriages, letting his fingers work as quickly as possible without his eyes. Just the other day, he made an eight-piecer as seventy-two carriages went by. Since 9 x 8 = 72, he decided that nine train carriages equalled each pentomino piece in that particular rectangle. It was as tough as patting your head and rubbing your stomach at the same time, and Calder felt in the mood for something hard.

Both Calder and Petra heard the rumble of an

approaching train. The engine appeared, and almost immediately Petra saw a sight that brought her to her feet.

A figure in a long, black cape stood in the window of what looked like an empty carriage. As the train flew by, he jerked the window open at the top, and the cape billowed and swirled around him. His fingers dropped a small object, and Petra thought she saw a fluttering of pages as the train sped on. All of this happened in less than a second, and the tracks were suddenly empty, the roar receding in the late afternoon light.

She was out of her front door and running towards Calder's house, three doors away, before she had stopped to think. She banged on the door, but there was no answer. She banged again, and soon she heard Calder's feet thumping down the stairs from his room.

In a breathless rush, Petra told him what she'd seen.

Calder jammed his feet into his trainers. Petra grinned, knowing this meant business, and suddenly the strangeness between them evaporated. As

they scrambled up the train embankment behind Calder's house, Petra couldn't help feeling happy that Tommy wasn't there too.

They weren't allowed to go up on the train tracks, but if they waited and got a parent to go with them later, the object could be gone. Besides, their parents might not want to bother – sometimes parents could be unimaginative.

Out of breath, Petra and Calder stood in the trees at the edge of the tracks. Another train was coming, but from the opposite direction. As it approached, the engineer sounded the whistle angrily.

'He's seen us. What if he calls the police?' Calder said.

'Hurry!'

Calder and Petra ran along the gravel at the top of the bank, heading north towards Petra's house. They found crisp bags, a swimming cap, a squashed shoe, cigarette butts – and then they saw it.

Chapter Six

NEW PENTOMINOES

A small book stood upright on its open pages, as if someone reading it had just put it down. Petra picked it up and wiped it gingerly on her shirt.

'Whoa!'

'What?' Calder asked.

'It's the same book I found at Powell's two days ago.' Suddenly spooked, Petra looked around them.

Calder nodded. 'Coincidence?' He smiled at Petra, an oddly wistful look on his face. Both kids thought back to the previous autumn, when a number of magical coincidences had led them to find and rescue the stolen painting. Collaborative problem-solving, that's what Ms Hussey called it – somehow, they'd been able to do things together that neither could have done on their own. As they slid back down the embankment to Calder's back garden, both were wondering the same thing: could three collaborate?

In front of Calder's porch, Petra dumped the dirt out of one shoe. 'Why don't you keep the book? Maybe we'll both read it.' As Petra said it, she heard the 'both', and realized it left out Tommy. She hadn't really meant to.

Calder flipped through the paperback, noticing tiny print and big words. 'No, thanks,' he said. 'You can tell me about it.' Calder stood in his front door as she walked away, and wondered why he hadn't asked her in.

Moments later, as Petra opened her front door, she wondered why she hadn't invited Calder to come over. She looked out at the empty street and thought suddenly about someone watching, but knew that was ridiculous.

Up in her bedroom she hunted through a pile of dirty clothes for the jeans she'd been wearing the day she picked up her copy of *The Invisible Man*.

She found the book in a back pocket, opened it to page one, and looked again at the words highlighted in orange: *an unheard-of piece of luck*. Then she opened the book from the tracks and flipped through the pages.

Orange marker leaped out at her from the middle of the book: *I remember myself as a gaunt black figure.*

The man on the train! Had he underlined the passage? Was he referring to himself? And had he also left behind the first copy, the one she found at Powell's?

Petra sank down on her bed and began to read.

⊞ ⊞ ⊞ Back up in his room, Calder ran his fingers through the orange pentominoes on his desk. He loved this three-dimensional set. They were a gift from an elderly neighbour, Mrs Sharpe. She had ordered them during the winter, but they were one-of-a-kind, and had only arrived last week.

Carrying this set was like having twelve shapes from the real world in his pocket. When he stirred them around, something he did all the time, he found that certain pieces made him think of actual places. The W felt like a set of stairs, the P felt like the end of the arm on his grandmother's rocking chair, the T felt like a small table, the N felt like a skyscraper stepping upward.

As he lined up the wooden pentominoes in a stiff parade along his window sill, the letters L, I, F, E, A, R, T popped back into his mind. He jotted them down on a scrap of paper. He could hear Ms Hussey's outraged voice saying, 'Plunder in the name of salvation,' and he wondered now if the Robie House was either a trifle or a filter. What an odd thought: was it unimportant, or was it something to look at the world through? He hadn't said anything about his Life & Art ideas to Petra in school today because Tommy had been there at lunch and it felt awkward, and then he'd forgotten to tell her on the way home.

Four of the seven letters were pentominoes – L, I, F and T, leaving EAR ... *Earlift*? Calder pictured someone with ears moved several centimetres up the side of his head. Tommy would like the *earlift*, and Petra would like the *trifle* and *filter* equation ... Calder sighed, for probably the fiftieth time in the last three days. When would Tommy and Petra get to be friends?

Suddenly a word in the middle of LIFEART popped out at him. FEAR ... and on either side were I and T, spelling it. Fear it, but that left out the L, he noticed with relief, so it must not mean anything. He looked again. Flare it ... well, that was clearly nostrils, he thought. He smiled again, wanting to pull both Petra and Tommy into this.

He heard heavy feet on the front porch, and the metallic slap of the letter box in the door as someone opened it and then let go. Tommy always peeked through the slot before ringing the bell. The buzzer rang now, and Calder went back downstairs.

'Hey, Tommy.'

'Hey. I found something weird.' Tommy had one hand in his shorts pocket. His knees were black with dirt. Calder knew what this meant and waited with excitement, thinking it was odd that he and Petra had just found something too.

Tommy pulled out a small, carved piece of stone that looked like a question mark without the dot. It had a fish head – or was it a dragon? – at one end, and tiny spirals all over the body. It looked old.

'Awesome! What is it? Where'd you find it?'

Tommy shrugged and grinned.

The two of them had spent many years scrounging and digging and sorting – Tommy doing the spotting, and Calder the organizing. Tommy had kept most of the finds. Calder hadn't minded – they were a team, and categorizing felt more interesting to him than keeping. When they'd both wanted something, Tommy was always generous.

'Wait till Pe—' As the words left Calder's mouth, Tommy's face shut down. The piece of stone disappeared back into his pocket.

'Come on, Tommy! She's smart, she really is. Why don't you like her?'

Tommy looked at Calder with his eyes almost closed. 'Maybe that's why,' he muttered.

'Not *bad* smart, she's *good* smart,' Calder added, realizing how silly that sounded. 'She's a buddy.'

Tommy shrugged. 'Gotta go. I'm working at Powell's this afternoon.' He slammed Calder's door behind him when he left. 'Oops,' he called out.

Right, Calder thought to himself. How could he ever have thought Tommy and Petra would get along? Balancing the two of them *stunk*.

Upstairs, Calder concentrated on his new pentominoes. Thinking about shapes always worked better than thinking about people, and being able to build with pentominoes in three dimensions was something new. They had been exciting in two dimensions, but they were amazing in three. If he ever ran a school, he'd have one room filled with nothing but large, squashy pentominoes. Kids would be able to pile them up, climb on them, even use them for spelling. And the playground equipment would be made out of solid combinations of the twelve pieces, designed by the kids themselves. Maybe even desks and chairs ... Calder pictured himself sitting on an upside-down Y and writing on a T desk. The possibilities were endless.

He hummed as he placed the Y on its long side then stood the T on the end of the Y, and braced the edge of the T with the I. Then he placed the V on top of the T. This was reminding him of something. But what?

Knocking the structure down, he played around again, this time closing his eyes and picking up three pentominoes. He opened his eyes and laid the L on its long side with its foot in the air. Then he put the F upside down on top of it, fitting them together in a sort of pyramid. The W went on top of the F, like a sideways M. Again, this felt familiar.

He knocked them down and started over. The W was a W this time, and leaned on one side. The L fit into the back of it, creating a stair with four even steps. The F lay on its side on top. He'd constructed a different shape, but it still stirred something in his memory. He picked up the N and scratched his head vigorously with it.

Determined to figure it out, this time he started with the F on its head. He built the W into the left side of it, and followed that with the L upside down on the right end. Again, he had a prickly sensation of recognition. Was it just that building with three-dimensional pentominoes would always remind him of something he'd seen before? Of course these shapes should feel familiar – after all, cities were filled with right angles and steps and overhangs.

He knocked the threesome down again, and stood the F up the right way. Then he slammed the table with one hand and jumped to his feet.

How could he not have seen it?

Chapter Seven

FEAR IT

As Calder pounded down Harper Avenue towards 59th Street, Petra stepped out on her porch. He had already passed her house and, watching his back, she could hear the faint clunk-chink of pentominoes bouncing in his trouser pockets.

Her mother had asked her to buy potatoes, but … where was Calder going in such a hurry? Petra jumped down her stairs in two steps and trotted after him. She wasn't spying, she told herself, just curious. Plus, it was blissfully still outside and a perfect moment for a detour. Petra loved this time of day on Harper Avenue, when late afternoon tipped into early evening and shadows from gardens threw giant blossoms and leaves across the pavement. She stepped off the pavement, avoiding a shape that looked like a man falling. Were shadows just accidents? Sometimes they looked like more.

Petra saw Calder pass the University School buildings, and head west towards the Robie House.

She peeked down 58th Street towards Woodlawn Avenue just as Calder stepped up to the low wall that surrounded the property. She watched him pull three pentominoes out of his pocket and stand them carefully on the top of the wall.

She waited until she wasn't out of breath and walked over.

'Petra! What are you doing here?'

'Out looking at shadows.'

Calder nodded. He knew Petra was great at noticing what most people hardly saw. 'Well, look: I picked up a handful of pentominoes, and it was these three, and they're Frank Lloyd Wright's initials! Not only that, I'm sure you can build sections of the Robie House with them. I ran over here to test it out.'

'Awesome!' Petra loved the way Calder thought with his pentominoes, and she watched as he experimented with several combinations of the F, L and W. She could see that the shapes echoed parts of the south elevation of the building with an almost magical precision. Could the pentominoes somehow help to save the house?

As she glanced back and forth between the house and the orange letter-shapes, she thought she saw something move in the first-floor windows. A delicate flicker of light darted through the criss-cross of triangles and parallelograms, travelling west to east in a clean, zig-zaggy line. It zipped down the three diamonds in the centre of each window, making the group vibrate in Petra's mind. She watched, transfixed, as the ripple came closer and closer, picking up speed, and suddenly – a puff of air knocked Calder's pentominoes over. Just as suddenly, everything was still again. Petra looked at the trees and the sky: no breeze, no clouds. She looked at the street: no cars to flash a reflection.

Her heart was pounding.

'Drat.' Calder's voice was muffled as he bent to pick up the pieces, wiping each one carefully on his shirt. 'Where did that come from?'

Petra was still staring at the windows, now quiet and empty. 'Those three diamonds in the middle of each window—' she began.

'The rhombi, you mean?' Calder asked without looking up. 'There's no such thing as a diamond in geometry. A rhombus is a parallelogram with equal sides.'

'Rhombi, whatever ...' Petra said, her voice trailing into silence.

Busy with his own thoughts, Calder said excitedly, 'If you had a collection of hundreds of these pentominoes, I'll bet you could build the entire Robie House, all but the window designs. Maybe showing that it could be built like a puzzle would even help to save it ...'

'Maybe,' Petra added in a whisper.

Calder looked over at her. 'What's wrong?'

'The building just knocked over your pentominoes. I mean – well, a light rippled through the windows towards us, and then there was that pouf. Out of nowhere.'

'Weird,' Calder said. 'You didn't imagine it?'

'I don't think so,' Petra said.

As they stood side by side looking at the house, an icy shiver ran down Petra's spine. 'I don't think the building wants us here,' she said.

Suddenly Calder remembered the words fear it, made up of six of the seven letters in LIFE & ART.

Fear what, though? This house?

Behind them, a familiar voice barked, 'Hey.' Both Calder and Petra jumped.

Tommy stood with his legs apart, his arms hanging stiffly at his sides. Petra stepped away from Calder and, although no one noticed it, the three now formed a perfect equilateral triangle.

Ignoring Tommy's unfriendly look, Calder told him about the F L W pentomino possibilities. His old friend looked a little less wary.

'That all you're doing here?' Tommy asked. His eyes darted nervously towards the garden.

Petra said coldly, 'I thought Calder's idea was cool. Plus, what is it to you if we're looking at the Robie House?'

Tommy growled something inaudible that sounded like 'tell me', and Petra backed away. She waved a hand and called out, 'Getting potatoes for my mum,' quickly stretching then snapping the unseen triangle as she turned a corner.

Henry Dare turned on his side, grunted with pain and rolled back. He stared at the ceiling in his hospital room. Good thing he wasn't an older man – that fall might have killed him.

A fourth-generation mason, he'd been hired by the university to take apart the house his great-grandfather had helped to build. It was an honour to have been given the Robie House contract; he was working on an important job, just like his great-grandfather, who had helped Frank Lloyd Wright. There was symmetry to the situation. One Dare had helped to put the place up, and another was helping to take it down. And now this.

'Something against nature,' he muttered to himself. 'I know what I know, and that house moved. No wet tiles, nothing, and it moved under me like—' He looked out of the window, thinking. 'Like a fish. As if I was standing on a big fish.'

When an impossible experience happens to you, he thought to himself, and you know you're not nuts, it changes how you see things.

And the child's voice: was it 'Stay away', or 'Stay and play'? There was a big difference between the two. At the time, he thought it came from inside the house.

Was the building trying to tell him that it didn't like what was going on? Didn't it understand? Now that he thought about it, there had been a series of accidents since he and the rest of the crew went in last week to measure and plan. A restoration carpenter had fallen down some stairs; another worker had been hit on the head by a light fixture; windows had opened and closed by themselves; the worker who found him on the balcony had suffered a broken finger when a French door slammed on his hand.

And what were those strange thoughts he'd had just before he fell, those thoughts about being young and alive and invisible? It was almost as if the house, knowing its fate, had heard his carefree thinking and become angry. Or was it that he'd touched the chimney, knocked a chunk of brick off, and kind of woken the place up?

These were crazy ideas, he thought to himself, shaking his head. Crazy ideas that for some reason didn't feel crazy.

As a kid, he'd loved magic tricks and could make small objects seem to appear and disappear. He could fool people. His great-grandfather had actually taught him a number of these tricks. The young man smiled at the memory of a disappearing card, a live turtle that could vanish, a spoon that bent ...

Deep inside, he wondered how his great-grandfather would feel about him working on this job. True, the house was a wreck, and true, the pieces were supposedly going to famous museums to be preserved for ever. But he could guess what his great-grandfather and Mr Wright would feel about the museum plan: both would be outraged. Henry Dare knew enough about the house to know that Wright had very carefully planned and balanced and scaled, so that no one part of the house could be seen without thinking of the others. The house was made up of many pieces, and they all fitted – almost like one of those three-dimensional brain-tickler puzzles. To even talk about taking it apart was sacrilege.

He sighed. If he didn't speak up, would somebody else be hurt? But who would believe him?

Chapter Eight

A GHASTLY FACE

Petra read for a couple of hours that night, unable to stop. She was surprised: *The Invisible Man* was a page-turner. Written in 1897, thirteen years before the Robie House was built, it had appeared a long time ago – before computers, before aeroplanes, before anyone in her family had come to the United States. She wondered if Frank Lloyd Wright had read the book.

The story began as a stranger turned up at an English country inn in the middle of a February snowstorm.

> **He was wrapped up from head to foot, and the brim of his soft felt hat hid every inch of his face but the shiny tip of his nose ... He staggered into the Coach and Horses, more dead than alive it seemed, and flung his portmanteau down. 'A fire,' he cried. 'A room and a fire!'**

Petra had no idea what a portmanteau was, but guessed it was a suitcase. She read on.

The stranger's arrival was the highlighted passage Petra had first found, the unheard-of piece of luck. Apparently the inn didn't have many customers in the winter. The stranger ordered food and waited in the parlour, but wouldn't take off his wet coat, hat or goggles. He didn't give his name. The innkeeper's wife asked endless questions, but the stranger didn't reply.

After she'd brought his food and left, the wife realized she'd forgotten the mustard:

> She rapped and entered promptly. As she did so the visitor moved quickly, so that she got but a glimpse of a white object disappearing behind the table. It would seem he was picking something from the floor ...
>
> 'Leave the hat,' said her visitor in a muffled voice, and turning she saw he had raised his head and was sitting and looking at her.
>
> For a moment she stood gaping at him, too surprised to speak.
>
> He held a white cloth ... over the lower part of his face ... so that his mouth and jaws were completely hidden ... all his forehead above his blue glasses was covered by a white bandage ... leaving

not a scrap of his face exposed excepting only his pink, peaked nose ... thick black hair, escaping as it could below and between the cross bandages, projected in curious tails and horns ...

Petra was jumping ahead now, reading faster and faster. She stopped to open her bedroom door and sat back down with her back to the wall.

The man was irritable and abrupt with everyone at the inn, who all assumed he'd had a terrible accident or an operation. That night, the wife 'woke up dreaming of huge white heads like turnips that came trailing after her, at the end of interminable necks, and with vast black eyes'. Despite how ridiculous the image was, a shiver ran down Petra's spine.

When the stranger's belongings arrived, he went outside, fully bundled, to see that the boxes got unloaded carefully from the cart. He was bitten on the leg by a dog, and rushed inside. Genuinely concerned, the innkeeper followed him, pushing open the door to the stranger's room:

The blind was down and the room was dim. He caught a glimpse of a most singular thing, what seemed a handless arm

waving towards him, and a face of three huge indeterminate spots on white, very like the face of a pale pansy. Then he was struck violently in the chest, hurled back, and the door slammed in his face and locked. It was so rapid that it gave him no time to observe. A waving of indecipherable shapes, a blow and a concussion. There he stood on the dark little landing, wondering what it might be that he had seen.

Over the next few days, the stranger shut himself in his room, ordered that he not be disturbed and set up what appeared to be a scientific laboratory. He went out at twilight to walk, and frightened everyone.

The ghastly bandaged face ... came with a disagreeable suddenness out of the darkness ...

Petra imagined what it might be like to turn the corner of Harper Avenue at night, outside Powell's, and come face to face with a bandaged, angry man who had no visible skin but the tip of his nose. She decided she'd had enough reading for the moment, and closed the book. How could something written so long ago be so creepy?

The Robie House was a bit creepy too – and old. Could she have found these books for a reason? Did Frank Lloyd Wright and the Invisible Man somehow fit together?

The noise and bustle of her family was a relief, and her mother smiled at her, surprised, when she asked if she could set the table.

By the time she'd played two games of Go Fish with her younger sister and helped one of her brothers make a tent out of his bed sheets, the man on the train had lost his importance for the moment, the spooky twinkle in the Robie House windows had faded and the Invisible Man had become just that.

Chapter Nine

THE BITE

Petra, Calder and Tommy didn't see each other that weekend.

On Monday, 6th June Petra stood outside her door before leaving for school. She took a deep breath. The sky was a cloudless, look-at-me blue and the temperature was perfect.

After the monochromatic cold of a Hyde Park winter, spring felt like an epiphany. Petra had just learned this word, and loved both the meaning and the sparkly, weightless sound – an epiphany was a moment in which there was a sudden flash of recognition, a yes. On a day like this, every detail felt deliberate and extraordinary: the velvety scent of damp wood and stone, the bright plink of purple and red and yellow blossoms, and the green underfoot and overhead, every vein and stem running like a river through the morning.

Her eye wandered to a cluster of pansies in the yard next door. The thought of the pansy description in *The Invisible Man* made her walk over and look carefully – silly, the idea of a pansy being frightening. She noticed that many of them did have markings that were like two eyes and a mouth, markings surrounded by a flush of cheerful colour. Each flower had five petals, with the markings on the lower three. Some looked like clover-shaped butterfly wings, or maybe abstract paintings done with a brush as thin as a hair. It occurred to her that the more you looked at less, the more less became more. Petra tucked this idea away for later.

Strange how much you miss when you're unhappy about something, she thought to herself. Well, nothing like Tommy would get in the way of *her* spring: writers couldn't afford to miss a second.

Petra saw Calder pop out of his front door and look in her direction. He raised his hand in a wave, something Petra noticed he didn't do with Tommy around, and walked quickly towards her.

'I told Tommy I'd meet him in front of the Medici Bakery before school,' Calder said.

'Sure,' Petra mumbled, wondering if he meant for her to come too. Despite her resolution of a

moment before, she felt the morning crumple and fade.

As she and Calder walked west on 57th Street, he told her all about the words that came out of LIFEART, including *earlift, flareit* and *fear it*, and she looked interested but distracted. She seemed excited about the filter-trifle idea in relation to the Robie House, but frowned. He noticed that her hair, which was thick and curly, was pulled back in a businesslike ponytail. It was actually more of a round puff than a ponytail.

Suddenly Petra said, 'You know the guy I saw on the train?'

Calder reached into his pocket. 'Yes?'

'He didn't have a face.'

'What?' *Clack-clack* went the pentominoes as Calder began stirring them.

'I couldn't see it, and I'm pretty good at those fast-glimpse train things. I don't remember blowing hair or a hood or anything – just the dark cape and the hand.'

'Weird when you think about the book cover.'

'Exactly.'

They had turned left on 57th Street and walked past blocks of buildings, Bixler playground, and were almost at the Medici.

'Petra?' Calder looked at her. 'Don't tell Tommy about the book, OK? He and I used to sneak up on the tracks, and ... well, he hates reading, anyway.'

'No problem,' Petra said stiffly. 'I read some last night.'

She was about to tell Calder about the highlighted passage in the second copy of *The Invisible Man* and to ask him if he thought the books could have anything to do with saving the Robie House, when Tommy stepped out of the bakery. He and Calder high-fived each other. Tommy immediately pulled off a piece of his chocolate croissant and offered it to Calder. Calder took a bite, and glanced at Petra as if to say: *It's good – have some!*

'Girls never eat this stuff,' Tommy said, nodding in her direction.

Petra stared at him. Was he serious? Was he implying girls only thought about getting fat? Or that she was fat? She turned towards Calder. He had stopped chewing, his mouth frozen in a shocked twist.

'Only girls like me,' Petra said angrily, then wished she hadn't said it. You couldn't *pay* her to touch that nasty kid's croissant. She spun around and began walking towards school. Neither of the boys called after her to wait up.

Tears prickled beneath Petra's eyelids. What was wrong with Calder? Why hadn't he said anything? She *knew* he was still her friend. Why couldn't Tommy try to adjust? What gave him the right to turn the clock back, to try to erase her?

As she walked, aware that her trousers were too tight and too short, she concentrated on not looking upset. *Luck, luck, luck, luck* was the rubbing sound her trousers made. Then she realized why, and suddenly felt a tiny bit better.

'*An unheard-of piece of luck*,' she muttered to herself as she pulled open the door of the Middle School. She held on to that idea as she slid into her seat in the classroom, determined to ignore both Calder and Tommy that day.

As soon as Petra turned away, Calder said

fiercely, 'That was *mean*,' and a large piece of croissant shot out and stuck to Tommy's arm. Tommy took aim and flicked the chewed piece of croissant back at Calder. It landed on his cheek, and Calder punched him. Both boys were half laughing now, half angry.

'But listen, it's because of the fish carving. I found it in the yard of the Robie House after school yesterday, and I wanted to ask you if you thought I should tell the class. That is, if we're talking about the house again.'

Calder stopped dead and looked at Tommy. 'Why didn't you tell me that on Friday when you were at my house?'

'Because you wanted *her* to be in on it.'

'Why can't she be?'

Tommy mumbled, 'She wouldn't understand.'

'How do you know? She would ... If you can't do stuff with Petra, you can't do stuff with me,' Calder said, surprising himself.

Suddenly Tommy took off. He headed at a run away from school and back towards his apartment building. Calder stood for a moment, looking after him. Great, he thought. Now both Petra and Tommy were mad at him.

Fine. Forget it! If they couldn't all three be friends, then maybe none of them should be friends.

Calder crashed noisily into his seat in the classroom, catching one pocket on the back of his chair. All of his pentominoes fell to the floor. Petra didn't even turn around.

Chapter Ten

DO NOT ENTER

That morning Ms Hussey was wearing a purple skirt with a yellow lining. She had new lavender flip-flops on, and her toenails were painted silver.

She stood in front of the class, her hands clasped together. 'I couldn't wait for you to get here!' she said, and they knew she meant it.

'I have a plan,' Ms Hussey began. 'We're going to visit the Robie House, as Calder suggested. We can't get in, but we'll just assume we're welcome to observe – there are times when it's important to act rather than ask. Your job is to figure out whether you think this building is a piece of art. If so, why? If not, why? We may be able to use your ideas to save the place.'

The class buzzed, pleased to be going on an unexpected field trip.

'Are we all here?' Ms Hussey said, scanning the rows. 'Where's Tommy Segovia?'

'I think he might be late,' Calder said.

Ms Hussey made a little mark in her attendance book. 'We'll leave him a note. So. The first thing I want each of you to do is get a clipboard, some paper and a sharp pencil.'

While the class rustled and rattled and sharpened, Ms Hussey wrote Tommy a note on the board, asking him to wait in the Middle School library until they returned.

Suddenly Petra wasn't mad at Calder any more. Had he left Tommy in a bush with a bloody nose? She hoped so.

'Let's be very quiet on the way out. If anyone asks, we're taking a spring nature walk.' Ms Hussey turned and led the way quickly out of the building. Petra loved the way she never looked back.

Petra would miss Ms Hussey terribly next year. Sometimes she made them do predictable work, like punctuation and arithmetic, but lots of times she kind of flew off in unexpected directions.

The sixth graders walked the three blocks to the Robie House without much talk, excited to be doing something that wasn't really allowed. As they approached the building, Ms Hussey stopped them.

'Now. You're going to be sketching and taking notes. The DO NOT ENTER tape is around the building and not the entire property, so you can explore as along as you don't cross that boundary. We'll meet back here in half an hour.'

Surrounding the building, the class peered in windows, walked through the garden and stood on tiptoe by the kerb to get a better view of the second and third floors. Soon they were seated singly or in small groups, drawing and writing.

Petra saw Calder looking closely at the west side of the house. He was standing in front of a raised terrace, and soon he sat down with his back to a tree, his clipboard on his knees. When she walked by, she saw that he was drawing three-dimensional pentominoes on a sheet of graph paper. He still hadn't said a word to her. But then, she hadn't said a word to him either. Maybe a break was a good thing.

Petra circled the house twice. Aside from the quick visit on Friday afternoon, she had never looked carefully at the place. This morning the windows were shimmery, almost like the tail feathers on a peacock, and the building itself looked maze-like, with four levels of walls and three levels of roofs. She had passed it countless times before, but had never noticed how complex it was.

What would it be like to live in a house like this? Bright and open, yes, but she thought she'd feel like a snail without its shell. Her house on Harper Avenue was tucked between the tracks and the street, and although it was noisy and crowded, it was cosy. The Robie House seemed more like a collection of shallow, open boxes stacked casually one on top of the other, some overlapping and some not. More like a place to play. The house was perfect for a game of hide and seek, a slightly creepy one.

As Petra continued to explore, she realized that she couldn't really see inside the house. The way the terraces and walls were set up, it was almost as if the windows were a tease, saying, '*Here we all are, but what can you see?*' There was something about the entire building that invited you in and at the same time pushed you away. Something that felt like a bit of a trick – or a trap. She wasn't used to studying art that felt uncomfortable.

She settled down to sketch outside the garage. The windows in front of her were smaller than some of the others, and the coloured glass that made up the design was particularly lovely.

As she drew, she had the odd sensation that tiny pieces of iridescent glass were changing colour when she looked away. Hadn't it been lavender-cream-ruby on the left part of the design? Not turquoise-sepia-ruby? She shivered, remembering her visit with Calder – the ripple of light and the strange breeze. And then something unexpected happened: one of the casement windows she was studying swung slowly open.

The window closed then drifted open twice more, and Petra guessed it must have been left unlatched. After all, Ms Hussey had told them that the interior of the house was in terrible shape and that the house had stood empty for over a year. Then, as Petra continued to stare, something dark moved inside the room. She felt the back of her neck prickle.

A shadow, she told herself, and then realized that to have a shadow you needed something solid.

As she hopped to her feet, the window clapped shut with a bang, as if someone inside had given it an angry pull. Petra snatched her clipboard and hurried around the side of the house.

Turning the corner, she practically fell over Calder, who was looking equally upset.

'There you are!' He grabbed her arm. 'Petra – I saw someone inside the house! A man with a cape.'

田田田 After a hurried whisper session in the corner of the garden, Calder and Petra agreed not to tell anyone, at least not yet.

Then they heard Ms Hussey's piercing whistle, the drop-everything-and-come signal, and at that moment a determined-looking man with a hard hat came out of the house.

He shouted, 'Hey! Stay on the pavement, kids! Whaddaya think the sign says?'

Ms Hussey was standing calmly on the kerb. As the class gathered, the man strode up to her and told her in a growl that a mason had fallen off the roof three days ago and was still in hospital.

Ms Hussey's face changed. 'Is he OK? What

happened?' she asked in a worried voice.

'He's conscious now, but not saying much. Came to take a look at the chimney, and went on-site before anyone else arrived. Probably curious, just like all of you, and must have slipped. The place is a deathtrap. When we went inside to get him off the balcony, I was hurt myself.' The man held up a large bandaged hand.

'Oh dear,' Ms Hussey said.

'The message, lady, is clear: the house is condemned. It's dangerous and coming down. Stay away!'

Up in his apartment, Tommy had seen the class coming. He had planned to forge a note from the dentist and go to school late. When the sound of kids' voices drifted through the open window, he peered out through the pondweed in Goldman's bowl.

At least Calder and Petra weren't walking together. But darn – he'd missed his chance to tell the class about his discovery.

He saw Calder sketching on the balcony. Several

kids appeared around the back of the house, under Tommy's window, but no one stayed there. He saw Petra stroll by without saying anything to Calder, and noticed that hair had escaped from her ponytail in funny black wings on either side of her head. Suddenly Tommy felt much better.

Time went by, and he dusted his shelf of fish treasures while he waited. Then he heard a sharp whistle and the kids all left. He'd wait a few minutes before walking to school. He knelt down by Goldman.

'I got something for the collection yesterday,' he said. Goldman swam closer to Tommy's nose, as if to say, '*What is it?*'

Tommy reached into his pocket and pulled out the carving. He held it in front of his pet, then lifted it up so that the head was directly over the water. The colour of white butter, the stone had little flecks of black in it. The mouth of the dragonfish was opened in a snarl, and Tommy poked the side of his little finger into the opening: the fangs were sharp.

'He's fierce, Goldman,' Tommy said. 'You'll have

to watch yourself.'

The tiny spirals on the creature's body turned in opposite directions, and must have been carved with a knife the size of a needle. Goldman came up to the surface and eyed Tommy's find nervously from both sides. Tommy, examining it also, wondered if it was OK to keep a treasure like this that had been found on a piece of private property. He hadn't told his mum about it, perhaps for just that reason. He'd hidden it under his pillow all night.

Something told him that the dragon-fish was an amazing discovery, maybe even the find of a lifetime. It reminded him of pictures in *National Geographic* magazine, but pictures from what part of the world? He squinted, trying to bring back the images, and thought he remembered a mountainous country with carvings that looked like this one. Maybe, when the Robie House was new and had rich people living in it, there had been a robbery and the fish was taken from a family art collection, dropped in the garden and then forgotten. It would be tough to research something like that, Tommy thought, imagining himself struggling through

pages of tiny print.

Maybe he could find an expert who would tell him about the fish. What were the rules on discovering art treasures of this kind near a deserted house? He'd heard about divers who recovered jewellery and money from ships at the bottom of the ocean and were allowed to keep what they found. Wasn't the Robie House just another wreck?

Maybe showing it to the class wasn't such a good idea.

On an impulse, he let go of the stone fish, and it fell with a quick plip into Goldman's bowl. Lying on its side at the bottom, Tommy was pleased to see it was almost invisible against the gravel. Goldman, after a quick dash around, took a dubious look at his new treasure, and then went back to gazing out of the window.

Chapter Eleven

THE HAYSTACK IDEA

When Tommy opened the classroom door, he was relieved to see kids all over the place. Some were writing, others were talking in small groups, still others were pinning sketches to a bulletin board at the back of the room.

Ms Hussey motioned him in, and absent-mindedly took the note he had written so carefully, in messy grown-up script, from his dentist. She stuffed it into her desk drawer, and Tommy took a deep breath.

He looked around for Calder but didn't see him. Then he noticed that Petra was gone too.

Tommy sat down at his desk. Ms Hussey came over. 'We went to the Robie House this morning,' she said.

Tommy nodded, sucking in his cheeks.

'Everyone is trying to figure out whether the

house is a piece of art. There are two columns on the board, YES and NO, and I've written some of the class's ideas up there.'

As Ms Hussey talked, Tommy noticed she had an earring with a tiny silver fish today, and that the scales rippled when she moved her head. Tommy wished it was in his collection.

He nodded again, and said, 'I live next to the house now.'

Ms Hussey's eyes widened, and she clapped her hands together, making Tommy blink. 'So you know exactly what the outside looks like! You see it in all lights ... that's fabulous. Grab a piece of paper and tell me whether you think it qualifies as a piece of art.'

Tommy looked at the board.

Under YES, he read:

- **Art should have surprises. The house looks like it's full of places to go in and out and change directions.**

- **Art should make you feel better. The house is bright and looks like it would be great to explore.**

YES

- **Art should make you think. The windows are filled with geometric shapes, and it must be amazing to look out from inside.**

Under NO, he read:

- **Art shouldn't be spooky. The house looks like it has a lot of dark corners.**

- **Art shouldn't be dangerous. This house looks like it has too many places for a kid to fall.**

- **Art should be a thing you want to live with. This house looks depressing.**

Funny ... he had thought the house looked really welcoming. Of course it didn't have any furniture in it at the moment, but he could imagine how much fun it would be to live in. A kid could peek out in all directions, with so many windows, and could even sit on the terrace walls or climb out on one of the roofs when no one was looking. And who had written that stupid thing on the board about falling? The place would be perfect for water pistol fights, and his mum would love all the space and sunshine. She'd be out sitting on one of the many balconies with her tea every morning.

So what should he add under the YES column?

He still liked books with pictures, and always remembered the illustrations that had hidden stories – the ones with a mysterious, slightly dangerous person or an open box you couldn't see into or a path that disappeared around a corner. He got up and walked slowly to the board. He wrote:

Art should have secrits. This house doz.

Ms Hussey came right over to him when he had finished. 'What secrets does the house have, Tommy?'

Suddenly he wished he hadn't written that. His handwriting looked crooked and young next to hers.

'Hidden treasure?' she asked.

Tommy turned dark red and looked at his desk. Could she read minds?

'Mmm, well, I meant art should stay interesting when you look at it again and again. And the Robie House keeps being interesting when I walk by it.'

'Good thinking,' Ms Hussey said, although she sounded disappointed.

The door flew open, and Calder stomped in, followed several seconds later by Petra. Both carried an armload of heavy library books. 'Wright info for sale!' Calder announced cheerfully.

On the way to her desk, Petra caught Tommy's eye. She winced as if she'd bitten the inside of her cheek, and both looked away quickly.

Ms Hussey put two fingers in her mouth and gave her everyone-in-their-seats whistle. 'What a day,' she purred, her purple skirt swishing as she turned quickly towards the board. 'Isn't it amazing how we can all visit the same place, at the same time, on the same day, and come away with opposite conclusions? From what you've said, not everyone thinks this house is a piece of art, although obviously we've only seen the exterior. So where do we go from here?'

Petra's hand went up. 'I think it's kind of spooky,

but I know some art is spooky. There are plenty of things in museums that you wouldn't want to look at every day. I think we should persuade them that cutting it up would be the same thing as cutting up a priceless painting.'

'Who'd believe that?' Denise muttered.

'Great idea,' Calder said.

Tommy choked. He'd never heard Calder say 'great idea' to anyone but him. He blinked rapidly. Pulling at the neck of his T-shirt, he told himself fiercely to toughen up.

'You wouldn't hack up one of those Monet haystack paintings in the Art Institute and sell the haystacks separately,' another kid added. 'Even if you didn't like the painting.'

Ms Hussey stopped walking and beamed at them. 'You guys are on to something. Comparing this kind of art to another kind of art may just do the trick.'

The class squirmed happily. Calder said, 'Maybe if we tell that haystack idea to the museum people who are getting the pieces of the house, they won't want them any more.'

'Yeah, like getting a cut-off foot in the mail,' Tommy blurted, and his voice sounded loud even to him. It was the first thing he'd said in a class discussion since he'd got back. There was silence after he spoke.

'Well, that's gross,' Denise said comfortably.

Tommy's shoulders stiffened.

'Not if you compare the house to a human body and the foot is a stained-glass window,' Petra said.

Tommy's eyebrows went up and stayed there.

'Making the people in charge think that way is pretty clever,' added Calder.

'It's not like the building is alive or anything,' Denise said in a condescending tone. 'Get a grip.'

Ms Hussey looked exasperated. 'Dramatic language can actually *allow* you to get a grip.'

'How do you know art can't be alive?' Petra said suddenly.

Denise rolled her eyes. 'Brick plus concrete plus wood plus glass doesn't equal a living thing,' she hissed.

Ms Hussey was looking out of the window, her head on one side. 'There are different ways of being alive,' she said slowly.

'Like being a nut,' Denise mumbled. 'And I don't mean a walnut.'

'Better than being a snake,' Petra said under her breath.

Ms Hussey, who didn't seem to have heard either comment, looked at the wall clock and clasped her hands together, signalling business. Her voice was crisp.

'See what you can find out about the house in the next couple of days. Notice all your questions as well as your answers – what you don't understand may be more valuable than what you do. Keep in mind what you saw this morning and all of your ideas about art, every single one. Maybe we'll come up with a wild plan. Who knows?'

Calder and Petra were loading library books into their backpacks as Tommy stood awkwardly to one side of the hall, his backpack swinging empty at his side. He looked at the floor, and out of the corner of his eye he saw Calder's and Petra's heads together, as if they were whispering, and then Petra's shoes approaching him. Everything in him wanted to run, but his body didn't move.

'Can you take some of these, Tommy? We have too many.' Petra's voice was nonchalant.

Suddenly Calder was standing next to him, too. 'Come on, Tommy. You have the perfect lookout. Let's work at your place today.'

As Tommy dropped books into his backpack, he thought he had never felt so relieved. Losing Calder would have been ... well, as bad as losing Goldman. And maybe he'd been wrong about Petra.

Just maybe.

Chapter Twelve

THREE!

The three marched in a horizontal line from school to Tommy's apartment. Calder was in the middle and did most of the talking.

As they passed a block-long lilac hedge, Calder waved his hand in front of his nose and said, 'Peuw! Too sweet!'

Petra said nothing.

Tommy coughed, as if to prove Calder's point.

'Anyone got any money?' Calder asked as the ice-cream van appeared. Tommy and Petra shook their heads.

'How's Goldman doing with his new view?' Calder asked.

'Fine,' Tommy said.

A silence descended, broken only by the occasional clacking and scuffing sounds of Calder's pentominoes and three pairs of trainers.

All were pleased to reach the Robie House.

'That's the one,' Petra said, pointing to a

casement window over the garage.

'What about it?' Tommy asked.

To his surprise, Petra told him about seeing the weird light in the windows yesterday, and about the window opening and closing this morning and then the shadowy shape inside the building. Calder told him about spotting something dark in the living-room area.

'Have you ever seen anything weird out of your window?' Petra said, startling him. Had she seen him looking out that morning?

His eyes narrowed. 'Maybe. Come on up,' he said, as if he had something big to tell them but couldn't do it out on the pavement.

Inside, the three dropped their backpacks in the middle of Tommy's room, which was also the living room. The apartment was cosy – two rooms and a pocket kitchen. Tommy whisked over to the window and took Goldman around the corner. 'Got to get him out of the way,' he said over his shoulder. 'Doesn't like visitors.' Calder looked surprised, but didn't say anything.

Petra went right over to the window and peered

out at the Robie House. 'Those rear windows are so complicated – all sizes, and in the oddest spots.'

When Tommy didn't respond, she admired the shelf with his fish collection. 'Calder told me you're an experienced finder.'

Tommy shrugged, 'I like to scavenge.' A terrible thought came to him: had Calder double-crossed Tommy hours ago and told her about the latest fish find?

'Frank Lloyd Wright was a collector too,' Petra was saying. 'I read it today. He bought and sold hundreds of Japanese prints, and visited Japan a number of times. The first trip was in 1905, just before he designed the Robie House. He was nuts about Japanese art and architecture, although he always said he wasn't influenced by it.'

'Really?' Tommy tried to keep the excitement out of his voice. A collector, just like him ... And the stone fish ... it actually did look a bit like things he'd seen in shops in Chinatown. Maybe Japanese art was similar to Chinese. Maybe he and Frank Lloyd Wright had something in common.

'Anyone want popcorn?' Tommy asked quickly.

'I'm starving.'

He hurried off to the kitchen and then realized, too late, that he'd left Calder and Petra alone, perhaps to say things behind his back. But if he invited them into the kitchen, they'd look at Goldman's bowl.

When Tommy returned with the popcorn, Calder and Petra were sitting cross-legged on the floor with books spread around them.

'So Tommy – what was it you saw?' Calder asked, taking a handful of popcorn. 'You know, out of your window.'

Tommy's mind raced. These days he seemed to be stumbling from one sneaky thing to the next. Suddenly he heard himself saying, 'I think it was a hand. In one of the upstairs windows.'

'A hand?' Petra asked, her eyes big.

'A kid's hand,' he replied. 'It waved back and forth, like this,' and he moved his hand in a slow fan movement, from side to side. He could feel Calder staring at him. Tommy opened one of the books that looked like it had a lot of photographs, and began turning the pages.

'Wow,' Petra said, looking from Tommy to Calder and then frowning slightly.

'So what's the plan here?' Tommy asked in what he hoped was an enough-of-this-silliness tone.

'Research,' Calder said abruptly.

The room was quiet for the next half-hour, except for chewing sounds. Petra picked at a scab on one elbow and took notes. Calder tore a piece of paper into strips and marked places in the books he was flipping through. Tommy picked up an invitingly slim volume called *Frank Lloyd Wright's Robie House*, and studied the old blueprints of the building. The outline looked like two long, narrow rectangles that had bumped up against each other and got stuck, one about halfway down the other. Like two barges.

Petra said suddenly, 'Hey. People used to think the building looked like a ferryboat, with that pointed terrace in the front. Like a prow.'

Tommy stared at her. Was it just an accident that they'd both been thinking about boats? If she could read minds, he was in trouble.

'Wow, this is *horrible*,' Petra squeaked suddenly.

Tommy heard Goldman, startled, take a quick, splashy dash around his bowl.

'The introduction says that every family that's lived in the house has had a huge tragedy. Listen to this: a guy by the name of Frederick Robie asked Wright to build the house. He wanted it to be a bright, modern place where his two young kids could run around, so he asked for lots of places to play. It looks like Wright pretty much planned the first floor for the kids, with a walled garden so someone didn't have to watch them all the time. They could run in and out on their own.' Petra paused for popcorn.

Calder said, 'I know, I read this cool part about how Mr Robie got his son a tiny car that he could drive around in the playroom and even out to the three-car garage where the real cars were kept. Awesome.'

'Wouldn't you have killed for that?' Tommy whacked Calder on the knee with the back of his hand.

'Absolutely,' Calder said.

'I've got pictures of the boy here,' Tommy added,

feeling better. 'He was the oldest of the kids.' The three of them looked at a picture of the young son, who might have been three, walking sturdily along a plank during the construction of the house.

'Dreamlike ...' Petra murmured, studying the rest of the photographs on the page.

'Look! He's on the south side, and the earth there is all torn up,' Calder said, glancing at Tommy. 'Must be lots of pennies, nails, who knows what else down there,' he continued.

Tommy scowled and pulled the book back.

The room was quiet again while Petra read silently. Then she said, 'So the Robies move into their perfect house, which cost them a bundle. Wow, Mr Robie describes it here as "the most ideal place in the world". And he also says "it seemed *alive*, because of the movement of the sun".' Petra paused to write.

'And then Fred Robie's elderly father died suddenly. Because Robie had once promised, long before he built the house, to pay off his father's debts, he felt he had to do it. It turned out they were enormous, and he went bankrupt overnight.'

'Boy, he got a bit of a bad deal,' Tommy said. 'Rotten dad.'

There was an awkward silence.

Petra nodded and continued: 'Mr and Mrs Robie broke up, and within a year the house had been sold. So that's the first tragedy.' She turned the page and read silently again.

'If they were wealthy they probably had a lot of stuff, and when they moved out in a hurry they might've dropped some,' Tommy mused.

Calder had taken his pentominoes out of his pocket, and was down on his elbows, squinting at a tall shape made from five pieces.

Petra went on, 'The next family was the Taylors. They had five boys. Here it says the boys were allowed to run laps from the end of the dining room to the end of the living room, "about thirty metres or so", and that twelve laps equalled a kilometre. The boys remembered loving the house—'

'No, really?' Tommy interrupted in a mocking voice.

'I'm just reading what it says,' Petra snapped, and went on, '*Another* boy was born after they moved in

– man, what a nightmare – and then Mr Taylor dropped dead suddenly. Within a year of buying the place! How do you like that?' Petra asked.

'The curse of the Robie House ...' Tommy whispered.

'Exactly,' Petra said, and Tommy closed his book happily. As she read on, she tried to tuck escaped hair back into her ponytail, then yanked the elastic out irritably. Using her index and little fingers, she loaded the rubber band on to her hand in a shooting position. Tommy noticed she did this without looking.

Black curls fanned out around her face as she said, 'So by November of 1912, two years after the house was finished, it had its third family. Now it's the Wilburs and their two girls. Mrs Wilbur wrote in her diary that six other families wanted the house when they bought it. Blah blah ...' Petra ran her finger down the page.

'Oh! The oldest daughter died in 1916. How awful. So that makes the second death in the house in six years. Whoa – that's one family disaster after another: divorce, then a dad dies, then a child dies.

'Wright visited the house at least three times while the Wilburs lived there. The youngest daughter said years later, in an interview, "I remember him well, his cape flying ..."' Petra glanced at Calder. 'A cape.'

Calder sat up.

Tommy looked from one to the other, and said, 'What's the big deal about a cape?'

Neither Calder nor Petra responded. She continued, 'The daughter also reported that Wright said, "This is the best example of my work." Wow. That was in the 1920s, after he'd built lots of other things.

'And here Mrs Wilbur says in her diary, "Frank Lloyd Wright called 4:30 PM ... and asked if he could see the house ... He wants to buy the house to live in & build glass extension on S. first floor." Strange he wanted to buy a house he'd designed for someone else, don't you think?'

Calder looked at Tommy. 'That's the south side, the garden area,' he said as he scooped up his pentominoes.

'I know that,' Tommy said. 'I don't think it's surprising he wanted to live there. Who wouldn't?'

Petra shut the book carefully. 'So, to sum it up, each family thought they'd landed in paradise when they first moved in. That's a lot of happiness mixed up with a lot of sadness. Three families, three sets of broken dreams.'

She looked towards the Robie House. 'Three again ...'

'Where'd you learn how to do that?' Tommy asked Petra. She looked surprised until she realized he meant the loaded rubber band. She shrugged and promptly shot him in the toe.

'Ow!' Tommy yelped. 'Cool. I've gotta master that one.'

After Calder and Petra had dropped books into their backpacks, Petra said evenly, 'Ever look out at night? With the lights out?'

'Kind of,' Tommy said, realizing he hadn't.

'Yeah, Tommy, you could really keep an eye on the place,' Calder said, pressing his nose against the screen. Late sunlight danced through leaves, dappling the brick on the rear wall.

'Sure,' Tommy said. 'Ghosts and all.'

'Ghosts?' Petra asked quickly. 'You sound awfully relaxed about it.'

'It's obvious, with all that sad history.' Tommy shrugged, as if the idea didn't bother him.

He heard a splash from the kitchen. Goldman was telling him to be quiet.

Then, as the kids gazed out of the window, an agonized moan floated out across the flat, bright light of late afternoon. Raw and dark, the sound felt imagined. It seemed to be coming from the house itself, from the bricks and glass and wood.

The three kids froze.

Petra was the first to speak. 'Did you hear that?'

Calder and Tommy nodded. It was hard to know what to say – sharing as a threesome wasn't exactly comfortable.

Petra found herself thinking, *I'm sorry that you're sad, house. You've lost so much.*

As the boys turned away she stood in front of Tommy's window for another few seconds, and it was then that one of the third-floor windows sparkled back at her. A three-part shape like a wrapped candy – two triangles on either side of a rhombus – became instantly, dazzlingly bright. Petra sucked in her breath sharply.

Three! The window seemed to signal back. *Three!*

A moment later, the glass was dark and still. That was for me, Petra thought to herself – but what was it?

Chapter Thirteen

A LINK

As Calder and Petra headed for Harper Avenue, Petra said, 'I think the house heard me thinking.'

Calder looked curiously at her. 'What do you mean?'

'You know that strange sound we heard. Well, I sent the house a silent message. I felt badly for it after everything I'd just read, and a window kind of answered me. This may sound crazy, but it answered me in threes.'

Calder stirred his pentominoes as Petra described seeing light catch the three rhombi in window after window on the first floor yesterday, and now the candy-shape on the third floor. 'I didn't notice the repeating threes so much yesterday until I saw the three today,' she finished.

'And I built structures that looked like parts of the Robie House with that group of three pentominoes, the F, the L and the W – as if those three jumped into my hand,' Calder added.

'And this all began on the third of June, the day Ms Hussey read us the article,' Petra said.

They walked silently for a minute or two, each sorting through their thoughts. Neither mentioned the three of Calder, Petra and Tommy.

'You didn't believe Tommy's story about the hand, did you?' Petra asked.

'He doesn't like being left out. And I know he thinks he missed a lot this year.'

'Yes,' Petra said, not unkindly. 'So he lied?'

'He might have exaggerated,' Calder corrected.

They walked quietly for a few more steps.

'He kept interrupting me,' Petra said. 'Like he didn't really care about the research. Is he always like that?'

'Sometimes,' Calder said. 'Petra?'

'Yes?'

'The pentominoes are doing strange things.' Calder stopped walking. 'I pulled out five in Tommy's apartment, and got the F, L and W again, just by chance, and the I and T. As I was building and listening to you read, I realized that I'd made a section of the Robie House wall and terrace, complete with a narrow casement window, and that I had added *The Invisible Man* to Frank Lloyd Wright's initials. Not only that, but they overlap. The W shape can also be the M. Like there's a link there. Crazy, huh?'

Petra stared at him, her mouth slightly open.

'Magical,' she said softly. 'What link do you think there is between *The Invisible Man* and Wright?'

'I don't know,' Calder said. 'Maybe just us thinking about the house.'

'Or maybe the house thinking about us,' Petra said slowly. 'Maybe there *is* a ghost, an invisible spirit attached to the house that made me find the Invisible Man books and notice the windows twinkling and the five petals on a pansy with three for the face. Maybe something is making you pick up—'

'Did you say the five and three of a pansy?' Calder asked. 'And the house is supposed to be pulled down on the twenty-first of June ... I think there's some kind of famous sequence that has those numbers in it.'

Petra grabbed Calder's arm. 'I wonder if

something from the house has tried to communicate with Tommy too, and he just hasn't known it?'

Calder's heart sank. The stone fish! Was there a message in Tommy's latest find? Tommy had told Calder that for some reason he'd kept digging in that one spot in the garden. He'd called it luck. Calder was dying to blurt out the secret of Tommy's fish to Petra, but knew he couldn't, not without his old friend's permission.

What had Tommy done with the fish, anyway?

Chapter Fourteen

ONE HUGE PATTERN

Calder phoned Tommy that night. 'Where's the fish?' he said immediately. 'Now that you and Petra and I are doing research, you've got to tell her about it.'

'Why?' Tommy asked.

'Why not?' Calder said irritably. 'Are you afraid she'll read up on it and figure out it's a treasure you can't keep?'

'Thanks a lot, Calder. You think she's the only one who knows stuff?'

'Of course not,' Calder said. 'It's just that we're trying to save this house, and every piece of the puzzle might matter. Who knows – maybe the fish is a clue.'

'What would a little stone fish in the garden have to do with saving a falling-down house?' Tommy asked, as if Calder was some kind of idiot.

'And why can't you and I have secrets together any more?'

'We can,' Calder said. 'But not secrets that don't make sense. I mean, if the three of us work together on this, we might come up with something. And finding an old carving in the garden is pretty exciting.'

'I don't see what it has to do with the house,' Tommy said.

'Fine,' Calder said, starting to feel angry. 'If you can't share, don't expect other people to include you.' He was thinking now about the Invisible Man books, and about how he'd been planning to tell Tommy about them.

'*Include* me? So you and Petra have secrets that you haven't told me?'

'Tommy! You're being such a jerk! I'm just saying that three brains are better than one. Or two.'

'Says who?' Tommy banged down the phone.

Calder sat still for a moment, looking straight ahead and not seeing anything. Why was Tommy being so selfish and pig-headed? He pulled his pentominoes out of his pocket and slapped them on the kitchen counter.

At that moment Yvette Pillay breezed into the kitchen, stopped, and said, 'Bad day?'

'Not really,' Calder said in a dull tone. Propping his chin on one fist, he began building. Echoes of the Robie House leaped immediately to mind. Moving the pieces, he recognized a section of the front terrace, then the balcony over the entryway. He smiled. Pentominoes were amazing, the way they chased the real world.

'Mum, isn't there a pattern with 3 and 5 and 21 in it?'

His mum closed her eyes for a moment then said, '0, 1, 1, 2, 3, 5, 8, 13, 21, 34, 55, 89, 144 and so on. They're called Fibonacci numbers. Why?'

Calder sat up. 'No special reason.'

His mum went on to tell him that Leonardo Fibonacci was a famous Italian mathematician who was born in the twelfth century, and did some extraordinary mathematical thinking.

'He helped to introduce our modern number system to Western Europe. He also discovered a sequence of numbers in which, starting with 0 and 1, each number is the sum of the two numbers before it. So 0+1=1, 1+1=2, 2+1=3, 2+3=5, 5+3=8 and so on. And the magical thing about the Fibonacci sequence is that the ratio between each of the numbers, as they increase, stays the same: 1.618.'

Calder nodded.

His mum went on, 'And that's not all: that ratio is called the Golden Ratio, and there's also the Golden Rectangle and the Golden Spiral. The Golden Rectangle is a rectangle that has a ratio of length to width that's 1 to 1.618. Many people believe that rectangles with these proportions are particularly pleasing. They've appeared in art and architecture for centuries, sometimes on purpose, sometimes just because they seem to turn up. You still with me?'

'I think so.'

'It gets weirder. Fibonacci numbers appear in nature, particularly in spiral shapes – leaves or petals that spiral, certain shells, pineapples, seed heads, even cabbage and lettuce. Wait—' She rummaged in

the refrigerator, then clicked her tongue in irritation and headed outside. Calder followed.

In the front garden, she bent over a clump of iris. 'These have three petals, and I know buttercups and pansies have five, and let's see ... marigolds have thirteen, and I think black-eyed susans have twenty-one. Many trees have branches that grow in Fibonacci patterns – 2, 3, 5, 8 and so on. Once you start looking for the sequence, it's hard not to see it.'

'Awesome!' Calder found himself thinking of the spirals on Tommy's stone fish. And of Petra's pansies. And how about the Robie House? Wright must have known about Fibonacci numbers.

After his mum went back inside, Calder stayed in the garden, bending over one group of plants after another. Sure enough, the 3, 5, 8 sequence was appearing everywhere – it was in leaves sprouting from delicate stems, even in the structure of veins in leaves. This Fibonacci guy identified one huge pattern.

'Lose something?' His dad's voice sounded tired.

'Hey, Dad. Not really,' Calder said. He watched his dad knock the mud off his boots and followed him inside.

Walter Pillay sat down at the kitchen table and rubbed his eyes.

'What's the matter, dear? How was work?' Yvette Pillay asked.

'I was just at the Robie House.'

'What were you doing there, Dad? Our class walked over this morning. Ms Hussey called the plans murder.'

'She did?' Calder's mum said. Appropriately enough, she had just stabbed the opening on a frozen pizza box with a large knife.

'She says that dividing the house up would kill it. We're trying to dig up any secrets about the place that could save it,' Calder explained.

Calder's dad unlaced his boots. 'The foreman told me about a mason who fell from the roof the other day. The man claims the roof kind of shook him off.'

Calder was all ears. 'Go on, Dad,' he said.

Walter Pillay looked at his son with a dazed expression. 'I was half listening to this fellow while I examined the area where he wanted to move a line of bushes, and suddenly I thought I saw the building expand and then contract. I mean—' He broke off and looked at his wife, who was frowning. 'The glass in the windows rippled as if it was flexible, as if it was the skin of an animal or reptile. I saw a – well, a wave of colour as all those little segments of glass moved sequentially.'

Calder stared at his dad.

Glancing quickly at her son, Calder's mum reached for three glasses and put them down firmly on the kitchen table. She poured three lemonades.

'You saw a bizarre optical illusion,' she said in her driest mathematician voice. 'It is an extremely complex structure. And, now, an unstable one.'

'Like the building breathed in and then out,' Calder said quietly.

Walter Pillay nodded. 'Exactly. My impression was that it took a deep breath and *sighed*. The man I was meeting with had his back to the building when it happened, and didn't see it. No one witnessed it but me.'

'Witnessed is a strong word.' Yvette Pillay had her head on one side, and her apricot hair caught the late afternoon sunshine, drawing a flowery softness into the kitchen. She looked pointedly at Calder, worried that he was a bit too interested.

'You're not going to help them, are you, Dad?'

Walter Pillay shook his head. 'No, I found myself saying that I wouldn't do the job.'

'Good.'

Suddenly Calder had an idea. Grabbing the phone book from the top of the refrigerator, he hurried upstairs and looked up the number for the University of Chicago Hospital.

'The mason?' a woman's voice asked. 'Who's calling, please?'

'A kid who knows something,' Calder said awkwardly.

'Just a minute,' the voice on the other end said, and Calder could hear a condescending smile in her tone. Why did some grown-ups always underestimate kids?

'Henry Dare here.' The voice was deep, and Calder suddenly felt young and shy.

'Ah, Mr Dare – I mean, my name is Calder Pillay

and my class and I are trying to save the Robie House, and I have something to tell you.'

There was a silence on the other end and then, 'What do you know about me?'

Calder wished Petra was with him – she always knew what to say. 'Well, that you fell.'

He felt himself blushing about the accidental rhyme. He sounded like an idiot.

'Yup, Jack and Jill time,' the mason said. 'A wicked tumble, but no broken crown.' The mason snorted. 'And no Jill.' He snorted again.

Why was the man talking in nursery rhymes? Did Calder sound that young to him?

Calder cleared his throat and lowered his voice as much as he could, trying to sound like his dad when he wanted to wrap up a discussion. 'Would it be possible for me to stop by after school tomorrow? I have a story that I think you'll want to hear.'

Mr Dare agreed to a short visit.

After Calder hung up, he gave the air a high-five, then patted himself on the back with a quick whack. He'd done it, and done it alone! Suddenly the possibilities felt enormous, and the faded light of early evening, which Calder usually avoided by turning on the lights, looked magical.

Should he ask Tommy and Petra to come to the hospital with him?

No, he'd do this alone.

Chapter Fifteen

GOLDMAN KNOWS

After Tommy hung up the phone with Calder, he looked miserably at Goldman, who was back by his window. Then Tommy kicked the wall, and the fish shot around his bowl three times, his eyes huge.

'Sorry to frighten you,' Tommy said. 'I was mad.' He noticed that Goldman had buried the stone carving without even being asked; only the tip of the tail still showed. Amazing the way Goldman always knew what was best.

Tommy's mum was folding clothes in the next room, having just come up from the laundry room in the basement. 'What, son?' she asked.

'Nothing. Just talking to Goldman.' Tommy sighed, and his eye landed on Petra's rubber band, which was still on the floor. He reached down and picked it up. Now how had she done that? He experimented with loading it on to his fingers so he could aim and shoot, but it was harder than it looked.

Zelda Segovia came into the room and sat down next to him. 'You look unhappy.' His mum always said what she thought, as far as he could tell, which he usually liked.

Tommy didn't know what to say. He looked out of the window.

His mum followed his glance. 'How do you like the new scenery? It's sad that the Robie House is going to be demolished, but I guess we'll be able to see it all happen from here,' she said.

'Ms Hussey said it was murder,' Tommy said. 'She wants us to figure out how to save the building.'

'Save it!' Zelda Segovia laughed. 'Well, that's a tall order.'

'Do you know any secrets about the place?' Tommy asked, being sure not to let his eyes wander to Goldman's gravel.

'Hmm ... Not exactly, but when I realized that our new apartment faced the back of the Robie

House, you know what I thought of? Funny, actually, that you mentioned murder.'

Tommy now looked directly at his mum. He liked to focus on her blue eye more than her brown eye. 'What?'

'A movie called *Rear Window*. It was old when I was a kid, but I adored it.'

'What's it about?'

'Oh, a man spends a lot of time looking out of the rear window of his apartment, a window not too different from ours, at other rear windows, and sees some suspicious stuff. But that's all I'll tell you,' his mum finished with a twinkle. 'Why don't you invite Calder and a couple of other kids over, and I'll rent a copy,' she suggested.

'Oh, that's OK,' Tommy said. 'But I'd like to see it, maybe just with you.'

'Great,' his mum said, standing up so that Tommy didn't see her slightly sad expression. There had been so many lonely times for her son over the past year, and she had hoped that coming back to the familiar world of Hyde Park would make things easier for him. It didn't seem like it had.

'How about tomorrow night? I'll meet you at the library after school,' Tommy offered.

'OK!' his mum said quickly, and ruffled his crewcut. 'It's a date.'

After dinner Petra took her backpack up to her bedroom. She pulled out the stack of Robie House books. Then, unable to resist, she picked up the copy of *The Invisible Man* that she had been reading the day before.

She decided to leaf through the pages, put her finger down and see what sentence she landed on. If Calder's pentominoes were talking to him, maybe the book would talk to her. Nobody could see her doing such a silly thing, and besides, there had to be a reason she had stumbled on this old book – not once, but twice.

Closing her eyes, she first ruffled back and forth through the pages, pretending she was shuffling a deck of cards, and then picked one page and one spot on that page. She opened her eyes. Under her finger was the line:

It was all like a dream, that visit to the old places ...

A dream! She had talked about the Robie House as a dream this afternoon, and visited it this morning. And here was a visit to the old places ... She shivered and closed the book, suddenly afraid of it. The story seemed almost to be echoing her life – or was it the other way around? And if it was the other way around, where was the Invisible Man? She pushed the thought away firmly.

And then she thought of her neighbour Mrs Sharpe. She had lived in Hyde Park for ever. Would she know anything unusual about the *old place*?

Petra went to the hall phone and dialled Calder's number.

'I have an idea,' she said right away. 'How about we visit Mrs Sharpe?'

Calder sounded uneasy. 'Well, maybe. But we can't go without Tommy.'

'So invite him,' Petra said flatly.

'I can't.'

When Petra didn't reply, Calder said quickly, 'I have an idea I'm following on my own tomorrow afternoon. How about you talk to Mrs Sharpe, and then we can compare notes. Private investigators in the real world don't travel around in clumps.'

On my own ... the words hurt. A million things jumped to Petra's mind, like, Why are you doing something without me when you know how well we work together, and How long have you had this separate plan, and Since when have we traded information like professionals? Aren't we friends any more?

All of this, she knew, was Tommy's fault.

Afraid her voice might get wobbly, Petra said only, 'Fine,' and hung up the phone.

She marched into her room, shut the door, and flopped down on the bed. She pulled out *The Invisible Man*, and read some more – better to be scared than sad.

The book was wonderfully distracting. Petra noticed that it didn't exactly tell you that the man was invisible under his clothing, but you got that idea bit by bit. As the story went on, the stranger became angry and violent, and crept around the village with no clothes on, once to rob a household for money. It was winter, and at times when the stranger was nowhere to be seen a loud sniff would come from thin air – he had caught a cold. Hours went by when he stayed in his room doing what he called scientific experiments, occasionally cursing and breaking bottles. Empty sleeves slammed doors, clothing floated around by itself, and a chair once flew through the air and chased the innkeeper's wife.

Again, Petra had to put the book down. The idea of a naked, furious, invisible man who could sneak around a house or a neighbourhood was definitely terrifying. And embarrassing.

But the idea of being invisible ... Petra could imagine the thrill of walking around without anyone seeing her. She'd be able to listen to conversations, read over shoulders, even slip inside the Robie House ... There could be an amazing power, a perfectly safe power, in being invisible. The thought was delicious.

Petra felt suddenly better, and called Mrs Sharpe, who invited her for tea the next afternoon at four o'clock. She told herself that going over there with both Tommy and Calder would have been too much anyway. Three was a crowd.

The words *too much, too much* washed back and forth in her head as she was falling asleep. Just like waves on the sand, she thought, or water sloshing in a bowl ... Suddenly she sat bolt upright.

Why had Tommy moved his fish bowl when they were visiting this afternoon? He'd been walking so quickly that the water sloshed back and forth, and she'd noticed Calder's surprised expression. That sneaky little kid was trying to hide something, she just knew it.

Tommy was hiding something that he didn't want Petra, and maybe Calder, to see. Something in the fish bowl.

What was it?

Chapter Sixteen

REAR WINDOWS

The next day at 3.46, Calder, Petra and Tommy each walked to a different part of Hyde Park, forming a scalene triangle that stretched rapidly. By 4.10, they had become the vertices in an isosceles triangle. A triangle of exactly the same proportions existed, oddly enough, in the Robie House windows, but none of the three knew that.

Calder knocked softly at the hospital door.

'Come in,' a man's voice replied, and Calder felt like running away. He now wished, with all his heart, that Petra was with him; she was better at talking. He stepped inside.

Henry Dare looked red and white and sticky, rather like a large stick of rock. He had bandages around his head and his middle, and perspiration on his forehead, which was deeply sunburned. He was younger than Calder expected.

'Sit, kid.'

Calder did, and resisted the temptation to stir

the pentominoes in his pocket. 'We're here about – I mean, I'm here about – well, a few of us were over at the Robie House yesterday, and well, we kind of saw the house *breathe*.' Calder's eyes were skating around the walls as he talked. His throat got very dry just before he said the last word, and he had to stop and swallow.

There was a silence from the mason. When he spoke, his voice was kind. 'Heard any stories about my fall?'

Calder's mind was now darting back and forth like a trapped mouse. Should he say yes? He decided he'd better not say another word. 'No, what happened?'

Obviously, he thought to himself furiously. Of course you've heard stuff, or you wouldn't be here.

Mr Dare turned his head and looked out of the window. 'It's like this, kid: I was up on the roof four days ago, and some strange stuff ran through my head. I was feeling kind of free and invisible up there, and just glad to be alive on that spring morning, and right after that the house twitched – like an animal or a fish or something. Like it knew what

I was thinking, and wanted to tell me who was the boss.'

'Invisible?' Calder repeated. 'And you said it twitched like a fish.' He and Mr Dare looked at each other.

'Sounds nutty, doesn't it?' the mason said.

'Not exactly,' Calder said slowly.

'And that's not all.' Mr Dare went on to tell him about the voice he thought he'd heard as he fell, the one that said either 'Stay away!' or 'Stay and play!'

'Will you be going back to work there?' Calder asked. This mason seemed like an OK guy. Calder wondered why he had taken such a nasty job.

'How could I go back?' Mr Dare replied, giving each word equal emphasis, then grunted with pain as he tried to sit up. Calder wondered if he meant *I'm not well enough*. Or had he meant *how could I go back to such a scary place? Or was it how could I work on a job like this?*

'How could I go back?' Mr Dare murmured again, almost to himself, as Calder closed the door.

Something bothered him about Mr Dare's story. The mason had mentioned feeling invisible, and he'd mentioned a fish ... And Petra had found *The Invisible Man*, and Tommy a fish.

Was this just a coincidence? Or had he stumbled on a small piece of a much bigger pattern, a pattern that might help to save the Robie House?

While Calder walked home from the hospital, his pentominoes rattling busily, Tommy and his mum settled down in front of the movie.

Rear Window was about a photographer with a broken leg who lived in a small second-floor apartment, a place that was almost exactly like the one Tommy and his mum were in now. It was summer, and very hot, and everyone's windows were open at night. Stuck in a wheelchair for several weeks, the photographer began watching the drama going on around him. One apartment belonged to a man and his invalid wife, and they could sometimes be heard arguing. And then, one evening, the photographer heard a sharp cry from behind the lowered blinds in that apartment. All night he saw the husband coming and going from the building with a heavy suitcase. At dawn he saw him washing large knives in the kitchen sink.

By then the photographer was truly curious and more than a little worried. The wife's bed was now empty, and the husband could be seen opening and shutting drawers in her room, packing a huge trunk.

Afraid that he might be the only witness to a murder, the photographer, in his window, continued to watch the man across the way, in his, and one tense scene led to another. By the end of the movie, Tommy had inched over until he and his mum were squashed together in a corner of the sofa.

'Wow,' Tommy said to her afterwards. 'I didn't know old movies could be that scary.'

'The director, Alfred Hitchcock, is famous for suspense. You don't see much violence, but you're on the edge of your seat. His movies are almost more about the power of what you imagine than the reality of what you see,' Zelda Segovia said.

Later that night, while she brushed her teeth, Tommy's mum heard scraping sounds of furniture being dragged across the floor. When she came in to say good night, she saw that her son had moved his bed directly in front of the open window, on the other side of Goldman's bowl.

She smiled. 'Watch out. You may become another Man in the Window. Sorry, Goldman: two men in the window. Better not turn that torch on – someone might see you.'

'That's exactly right,' Tommy said quietly, peering out into the darkness. He lay awake for some time, watching light ripple across the segments of glass in the empty rear windows of the Robie House each time a car went by. Inviting, that's what the house was. Tommy tried to imagine what the kids who lived on the third floor, so many years before, might have seen when they looked out through those patterns. A world of triangles and parallelograms? Not the bedroom he was lying in, that's for sure. His building hadn't even been built yet.

He heard a quiet, uneven tapping, as if a woodpecker had got up too early and was doing a careless job. This was followed by a metallic clink, a thud, then silence. Leaning on his elbows now,

Tommy squinted at the house. He looked hard at the third-floor windows he had just been thinking about, and couldn't help remembering his lie about the hand waving like a fan. What if it appeared? What if it waved to him right now?

To his relief, all was dark glass, brick, and the hint of flowers in a breeze pulling through the neighbourhood like an unseen current. As if in response to the thought of water, Goldman took another lap around his bowl. Tommy lay down again, thinking that even though things weren't as great as they used to be with Calder, it was good to be back in Hyde Park, good to be sleeping next to Goldman on this spring night, and good to be watching the rear windows of a house that felt so much like a home.

Felt, he wondered drowsily to himself. I've never been inside the place – how do I know what it feels like? He didn't allow himself to wonder for even a second if he knew what a home felt like.

The best collectors are also travellers, he reminded himself. They take their homes with them. They live in many different places, and that's the way they like it.

Tommy was fast asleep when the tapping began again. Neither he nor Goldman heard it.

Chapter Seventeen

PART OF THE ART

Mrs Sharpe lived around the corner from Harper Avenue, by herself, in a big house that she had been in for almost fifty years. As Petra stood on the front porch that Tuesday afternoon, she wished with all her heart that Calder was with her. The two of them had had tea with Mrs Sharpe several times during the past winter, when they'd been working on finding the stolen painting, but Petra had never visited her alone.

The door flew open the instant Petra rang the bell, and Mrs Sharpe said in an icy tone, 'Hurry up, girl. You're letting the cool air out.'

Passing lush oriental rugs and walls covered with paintings and books, Petra followed her elderly neighbour into the kitchen. Mrs Sharpe's house smelled like furniture polish and chocolate. She had baked cookies just for Petra, and on a warm day! Mrs Sharpe was full of surprises, Petra thought fondly. You could never quite relax around her, but

Petra didn't mind. After all, Mrs Sharpe had at least four ideas behind her back for every one that you saw up front. She was a thinker and, as Ms Hussey had once said, thinkers shouldn't have to be predictable. Today she was wearing a silk dress that reminded Petra of a ripe plum, and her white hair was twirled neatly into its customary bun.

After she had poured them each a glass of iced tea with mint and Petra had eaten two warm cookies, Mrs Sharpe said, 'So. How's the sleuthing business?'

'Well, our class visited the Robie House yesterday.' Petra knew that Ms Hussey and Mrs Sharpe had become friends the previous autumn.

Mrs Sharpe nodded her approval. 'Ah. So that's why you're here. This plan is a dreadful end to an extraordinary piece of art.'

She ran one bony finger down the side of her glass, leaving a trail through the condensation. 'In 1955 there were thirteen of us living in the house, all students. I was only there for several weeks, while they completed a University of Chicago dormitory, but it was an experience I've never forgotten.'

'You *lived* in the house?' Petra squeaked. 'You were a student here?'

'Art history,' Mrs Sharpe said drily. She looked at her lap for a moment, as if waiting for a fly to stop buzzing. Petra held her breath, determined not to interrupt again.

'Living in that house felt a bit like living in a slowly turning kaleidoscope – the light captured by those windows changes by the hour and sometimes even by the second, and yet what you see always fits perfectly with everything else. It's almost as if Wright managed to set up a resonance between the structure itself and all of the details – art glass, ceiling grilles, rugs, lamps, balconies – that changes continuously and yet remains seamless. I'm not sure anyone has ever been able to figure out exactly how he did it. A symphony, that's what the place is like – a complex Bach symphony that sharpens your mind even if you can't comprehend every strand of harmony. And when you stand inside, it's almost as if you become part of the art yourself, an instrument in Mr Wright's hands. There's the feeling of belonging to someone else's imagination.'

Mrs Sharpe had a faraway look Petra had never seen before. She knew Mrs Sharpe liked to write, and now Petra knew why – her words fitted gracefully and cleanly, in an *of course* kind of way, when she put them together. Petra was glad that the boys weren't squeaking chairs or crumbling cookies next to her.

Almost as if she'd forgotten Petra was there, the old woman continued, 'Wright had a difficult personal life, and many people thought he was arrogant. He was a bit of a puzzle himself, a complicated person who could somehow make impossible situations look like they weren't what they were.

'I once heard a story about Wright having lost an object of his own on the property during construction, a talisman of some kind, something that meant a great deal to him. And then years later he bent over backwards to save that building twice from demolition. But now he's no longer here to do it ...' Mrs Sharpe's voice lost its dreamy tone and she looked at Petra with a twinkle. 'At least, we don't *think* he is.'

Petra looked back at her, but couldn't quite

smile. What was she talking about? Wasn't Wright dead? And what was a talisman?

'Calder and I saw something odd in the windows of the house yesterday – kind of a shadow and then a light that ran through the glass and blew Calder's pentominoes over.' Petra's words hadn't come out right – it all sounded silly, but Mrs Sharpe didn't laugh.

Her voice soft, she said, 'Yes, those windows communicate. And I've heard stories over the years about people and odd lights being seen in the house at night. Ghosts wouldn't be surprising, given the history of the place. Having been built for a family, and for children in particular, its fate has been all wrong.'

Petra nodded silently, her mind racing. She said, 'Have you seen any ghosts?'

She fully expected Mrs Sharpe to close the topic with a bang, but to her surprise she said in a matter-of-fact tone, 'Not there.'

'Oh,' Petra said, hoping she wasn't going to stop. 'Umm – where?'

Mrs Sharpe pushed the plate of cookies towards

Petra, and she obediently took another.

Then Mrs Sharpe said, 'Something I saw one summer when I was about your age. We were on Nantucket Island, in Massachusetts.'

Petra put down the cookie. She remembered now that both Mrs Sharpe and Ms Hussey had family from Nantucket. Did Ms Hussey know this story?

Mrs Sharpe went on, 'My parents had rented an eighteenth-century house on the edge of a graveyard. There were latch doors that opened on their own, and sometimes we heard footsteps, but I don't remember feeling scared. People on the island are matter-of-fact about ghosts. The fog, oddly enough, frightened me more – every evening it surrounded the house, swirling and drifting and catching in trees, and then there was the mournful sound of the foghorn.'

Petra shivered, but Mrs Sharpe didn't seem to notice.

'I slept by myself in a bedroom on the first floor. One night I awoke to see the shadowy figure of a young girl kneeling in a corner of the room. She seemed to be struggling to pry up a floorboard. I remember her hair was in plaits, and she wore what looked like a long, loose gown. She didn't seem to know I was there, even when I made a noise, and she finally faded and disappeared.

'My first instinct was to try to help her. In the morning, my sister and I lifted the wide board where she had been kneeling. There were dead spiders and thick cobwebs as if nothing under the floor had been disturbed for a long time, and beneath that was a little notebook bound in leather.'

Mrs Sharpe got slowly to her feet, held up one finger, and left the room. When she returned she had something in her hand.

The leather was dry and desiccated.

The paper was wavy and the ink inside had run until the words were mere blobs and stains.

'Oh, how tragic!' Petra burst out. 'Nothing you can read!'

'Impossible, sad to say. Paper must have been soaked.' Mrs Sharpe looked tenderly at the little book.

'And you *took* it?' Petra asked.

'I thought maybe she wanted me to. But I did put something back under that board – my copy of a book called *The Invisible Man*. I remember it made some uncomfortable ideas seem very real, and to this day I can't look at a pansy without thinking of it.'

'What?' Petra squawked. 'Pansies! I'm reading it right now! *The Invisible Man*, I mean.'

Mrs Sharpe raised one eyebrow, as if the coincidence wasn't a surprise. She said calmly, 'I wanted to give the ghost a message, to let her know that I believed she was real – sometimes visible and sometimes not.'

'Why do you suppose I found *The Invisible Man* just before you told me this story?' Petra asked.

Mrs Sharpe was standing now, signalling that the visit was over. 'Good luck in your work on the Robie House,' she said stiffly.

'But – I was going to ask you about whether you knew any secrets that might help to save the house,' Petra said quickly.

'How many secrets can you learn in one day?' Mrs Sharpe said in a cryptic voice. 'I think you have everything you need.'

After the door closed, Petra stood outside for a moment, blinking in the late afternoon sunshine. Perhaps it was the cookies and sugary iced tea, but her mind felt like a runaway ping-pong ball. On the walk home, she bounced from ghosts to *The Invisible Man* to Frank Lloyd Wright making a walk-in kaleidoscope and leaving a tali-something behind him ...

Suddenly, as she passed Calder's house, she looked down at new cement filling a cracked section of the pavement. Five lines looked almost as if they spelled I M – a kid scratching with a stick, she told herself, but the words *Invisible Man* ricocheted back and forth in her mind.

How many secrets can you learn in one day? I think you have everything you need.

Everything I need, Petra thought to herself. What has Mrs Sharpe given me? And why wasn't she surprised about Petra reading *The Invisible Man*?

Was this just a coincidence?

Chapter Eighteen

SACRILEGE

Ms Hussey could barely be seen the next morning as she opened the classroom door. Balanced on one shoulder was a hefty stack of poster board, and on the other a gigantic cardboard tube. Hanging from one arm was a bucket of scissors. A plastic bag filled with bottles of glue hung from her belt. Her sixth graders rushed to help her unload.

She had her *I've got a secret* look and wouldn't answer questions until the class was seated.

'After you left school yesterday, I realized that we need to do exactly what you suggested – destroy some paintings. I rushed downtown to the Art Institute store, and when I told them you kids were trying to save the Robie House by doing this project, they practically gave me thirty different posters of famous works in their collection. This morning I borrowed the rest of these supplies from the art room. Note the scissors and glue. Now what exactly do you think we're going to do?'

'Cut and paste!' shouted a delighted voice.

'Back to kindergarten,' mumbled Denise.

'I get to choose first!'

'No, me!'

Ms Hussey's hands went up as if she were stopping traffic. 'What's this about?'

'Chopping up art, of course,' someone piped up.

'Right,' Ms Hussey beamed. 'Sacrilege. Desecration. Appalling destruction. First we all glue the posters to the cardboard so that they're stiff. Then I thought each of you could pick one image and cut a vital chunk off the side of it, the worst chunk you can imagine, so that it's clear that you've done a terrible thing. Then ...' Ms Hussey paused. 'Then I'm not sure what the next step should be.'

'No!' Tommy's voice was awkward and excited, and everyone looked at him. 'I mean, we should cut this stuff up *in front of* the people we want to upset. You know, the murder idea – seeing a haystack being cut off is worse that seeing the painting in two pieces afterward. It's more violent.'

Calder's pentominoes were already on his desk. 'Tommy's right,' he said. 'Make them witness it!'

'Cool!'

'Art blood-and-guts!'

Ms Hussey looked around. 'I don't want us to get gruesome here, but I have to agree. It's an extraordinary action,' she said slowly. 'After school today I'll call press, TV, anyone who will record this, and let them know that a group of Hyde Park children have a plan to save the Robie House, and that there will be a public event. This kind of attention is the very thing that could bring in the money to save the house.

'We only have three more days of school, but I'm sure we can be ready by tomorrow. You could all stand on the pavement in front of the house, each with a painting in hand, and then start in with the scissors, one of you at a time so that we get the full horror of the idea.'

By the end of the morning, a stack of famous images leaned against the blackboard. Georges Seurat's *A Sunday on La Grande Jatte* was next to Edgar Degas' *The Millinery Shop*, Edward Hopper's *Nighthawks* was next to Pablo Picasso's *Man with Moustache, Buttoned Vest and Pipe*, and Henri Matisse's *Woman Before an Aquarium* sat near Gauguin's *Polynesian Woman with Children*. The door opened at one point and the principal, who was leading a tour for prospective parents, looked around with a puzzled expression and murmured to the group, 'We're big on art here.' The sixth graders nodded cheerfully. As the door closed, Ms Hussey winked at them.

While the class peeled dried glue off elbows and knees, she said, 'Can you keep a secret?' There was a roar of yeses.

'For now, not a word to anybody about what we're going to do. Got it? I know it's difficult, but sometimes it's important to withhold information.'

Tommy swivelled in his chair and looked triumphantly at Calder, who stuck his tongue out. Both were thinking about the stone fish.

'But what if someone official finds out we're planning this? Can they stop it?' Petra asked in a worried voice.

Ms Hussey shook her head. 'I think we'll be OK as long as we don't cross that Do Not Enter tape. Plus, there will be press watching, which usually makes any bullies behave better. And kids, as we all know, never do anything wrong.' Ms Hussey smiled beatifically.

The class could hardly wait.

Thursday, 9th June was exactly what the sixth graders had counted on: clear and warm, with a thoughtful breeze. It was an ideal day for a demonstration.

As the class marched around the corner of 58th Street, headed for the Robie House, they stopped momentarily when they saw the TV cameras and the parked vans with press and newspaper lettering along the sides. Ms Hussey turned around and called softly, 'Don't let them see you're nervous!'

A crowd of at least sixty people had gathered in the street around the house, and police, who had been informed ahead of time, had blocked off the area with sawhorses. Parents had all been invited, and many could be seen peeking over the heads of press.

The sixth graders stood in a long, straight line in front of the house. Each held up a large painting.

One by one, they stepped out of the line and introduced themselves and the piece of art they were holding. Ms Hussey had told them to say whatever they wanted about it.

When Petra stepped forward, she said, 'I'm Petra Andalee, and this is Henri Rousseau's *The Waterfall*. He painted it in 1910, the same year the Robie House was built. I like this painting because it's jungly and mysterious and the leaves and plants seem almost like they're breathing. If I do this to it – ' she paused and hacked vigorously at the painting, cutting two people in half, ' – does this change what you see? Do I have two pieces of art, or one crime?'

Calder held up a square, abstract painting. 'I'm Calder Pillay, and this painting was made in 1935 by Piet Mondrian. As you can see, it's all rectangles divided by black lines. There are two grey rectangles, one small red one, and the other eleven are white. Every rectangle is a different size, and there is something very perfect about the way they fit together. A lot of the Robie House is made of careful rectangles. If you cut the painting like this – ' Calder paused to chop his way across the poster board, ' – do you think it's the same? Of course not. And if the Robie House is cut up ...' Calder paused. 'It's easy to imagine what a waste it would be.'

Other sixth graders explained that they liked the people having a summer picnic on an island, then cut a jagged line separating the group, or that they admired the woman dressed in the ballgown before she lost her head, or that they liked the beach scene before the water was cut out.

The testimonials and the destruction rolled on, and the only sounds coming from the crowd were an occasional gasp or sniffle. It was, as Ms Hussey had anticipated, a memorable and moving sight.

When it was Tommy's turn, he said, 'I'm Tommy Segovia, and I've grown up mostly in Hyde Park. I think the Robie House is a piece of art just like this painting by Vincent Van Gogh. It's called *The Bedroom*, and he painted it in 1889. I like it because it's comfortable and has blue walls, a green floor, two yellow chairs, a red blanket, an open

window, and everything's at a crazy angle. If I cut the room in half, look what happens.'

Tommy hacked away and then held up the two pieces of the image. 'Destroyed. Why is this any different from cutting up Frank Lloyd Wright's art? The Robie House was built to make kids happy, and the kids who lived in it never forgot it. They loved all the sunshine, and they loved running in and out and up and down. People say it's a building that feels kind of alive, and we think so too, and if you don't try to save it, you'll be witnesses to a – ' he looked hesitantly at Ms Hussey, then plunged on, ' – to a murder.'

There was a stunned silence, and then someone began to clap. Soon it seemed like the entire crowd was applauding, press and all. Tommy looked dazed but happy, as if he wasn't sure where all those words had come from. Kids in the class patted him on the back and picked up the pieces of their posters and waved them in the air.

As the class headed back towards school, Tommy could barely feel the ground beneath his feet. Sixth graders who hadn't said a word to him since he'd returned were being friendly. Even Denise smiled at him. He sucked in his cheeks so many times that morning that they hurt.

Petra, walking by the side of the house, found herself thinking, *See? We kids care. We won't give up on saving you.* Looking at the empty windows, she felt a bit frightened by her own promise. Could she keep it?

Calder, glancing back at the house, saw Henry Dare on the corner with a cane. He wanted to wave, but the mason's head was turned. Had Mr Dare listened to their speeches?

Just then Calder thought he heard a silvery voice, a voice with a slight echo, coming from the garden by the house. 'Stay and play!' were the words that drifted through the morning light. Wasn't that what Mr Dare had heard when he fell? Calder looked around quickly, his heart pounding, but no one else seemed to have heard.

When Calder glanced up once more, the Robie House windows looked dark and sad, reflecting back only the shiny yellow of the Do Not Enter tape.

The demonstration had been a triumph. On the front of the *Chicago Tribune*, the next morning, was a picture of Tommy Segovia holding up half of the Van Gogh, his mouth wide open. *A Murder is Announced in Hyde Park*, the headline said. Tommy couldn't wait to get to class.

As he hurtled around the side of the Robie House on his way to school, a man in construction gear stepped over the yellow tape into the middle of the pavement. Tommy was just trotting around him when he said, 'Hey! You the kid in the paper?'

Tommy nodded and grinned, ready for praise. He'd seen his class on the news last night, heard them on public radio, and now seen himself on the front of one of the biggest newspapers in the United States.

'I wouldn't be so proud of myself if I was you,' the man growled. He had glasses with a heavy black rim and thick lenses – his eyes looked small and mean. Startled, Tommy took off at a run, something his mum had taught him to do if he ever found himself alone and in a situation he didn't like.

At the end of the block, he looked back and was startled to see the man still standing on the pavement. Arms crossed on his chest, he scowled in Tommy's direction.

田田田 As sixth graders high-fived him all morning, Tommy forgot about the nasty exchange in front of the Robie House. He'd never felt as popular.

At lunchtime Ms Hussey, looking like a happy rose in layers of pink, made an announcement: she had just heard from the Principal's office that a group made up of the Mayor of Chicago, an official from the National Trust for Historic Preservation, the President of the University of Chicago, and several big-shot lawyers were going to be visiting and evaluating the house next week.

'Although school will be out by then, this is thrilling news,' she said. 'Mission partially accomplished: we've attracted attention and now, if the house is pulled apart, the museums involved will have to think carefully about what they're accepting.'

To celebrate, Ms Hussey ordered pizza for lunch, even though that was supposed to be the prize when the paper feet completed their march around the classroom walls. As she said, the class had covered more important ground.

She didn't seem to mind that they hadn't finished the last twenty pages of the spelling or maths book, and that they'd worked on nothing but Robie House ideas for the last week.

Tommy was beginning to think that Ms Hussey was one awesome teacher, and that fighting for the Robie House might be the best thing that had ever happened to him.

He wasn't going to give up.

Chapter Nineteen

RED HERRINGS

School ended for the year on Monday, 13th June.

The transition from school into summer was always bittersweet for Calder. Freedom to do what he wanted and the weeks of unplanned days and no-homework nights were all good, but his household was quiet. During July and August the neighbourhood felt *too* peaceful to him; university students left, and many kids went off to camp. Calder's parents didn't believe in camp. And then there was Petra and Tommy, who would both be home too. Calder wasn't sure this was a good thing.

On the last morning of school, kids cleaned out desks and lockers and filled carrier bags with old papers, half-dead erasers and notebooks. Lost gloves materialized, and overdue books went back to the library. Before dismissal, Ms Hussey called everyone together in the back of the room. The sixth graders sat on the floor in a large circle.

'Before you leave, I'm going to pass around my Lucky Stone.' The grey rock that always sat on her desk now filled the palm of her hand.

'I found it on a beach I loved, when I was about your age. I guess you could say it's kind of my talisman – you know, an object that has magical powers, that can hear your wishes and dreams. Some people believe a talisman can protect you.'

Petra's eyebrows went up – so that's what a talisman was! First Wright had one and now Ms Hussey ...

'When you get the stone, close your eyes and make a wish. Don't tell anyone else what you've wished for. But before we do this, I need to say two things: one, know that you have tremendous powers within yourself, even if no one else can see them, and two, know that you can't always see the results of your actions. What you've begun for the Robie House will undoubtedly change the destiny of that piece of art. Be patient, and know you did the best you could. This is a house that has powers of its own.'

As the stone passed from hand to hand, the class was silent. Some kids smiled as they held it, or looked around the room as if they needed an idea for a wish. When Tommy got it, he closed his eyes so tightly that he saw spots. When Calder held it, he stared at his pentominoes pocket while he made his wish. When Petra had it, she squeezed the stone for so long that the next kid whispered, 'One wish,' and Petra glared at him.

The day ended just before lunchtime. It was difficult saying goodbye to Ms Hussey, and there were shaky voices, ducked heads and long hugs.

Calder stirred his pentominoes noisily as he hopped down the stairs on his way out of the building.

'Wait up!' said Tommy.

Petra caught up too, and walked on the other side of Calder. When she suggested they make sandwiches at her house and take them up in the Castigliones' tree house, the boys agreed.

As they left school and headed towards Harper Avenue, a hot wind swept runaway papers in angry swirls across the playground and summer began beneath heavy clouds.

Not wanting the boys to look at the seat of her trousers as she climbed, Petra waited until they were both up the ladder, one carrying the root beer and the other three peanut-butter-and-jelly sandwiches. Then she stuck her pencil behind one ear and, holding her notebook in her teeth, started after them.

A weathered structure that filled much of a maple tree between Petra's and Calder's houses, the tree house was a small, enclosed shelter with one window and a trapdoor. Twelve boards nailed to the tree trunk formed a ladder. The Castigliones' kids had left home years before, but the tree house lived on.

The three kids had walked back to Harper Avenue from school without a lot of talk, and made sandwiches with even less. Now as they settled awkwardly into the small space up in the leaves and ate their lunch, both boys waited for Petra to say something.

She raised her paper cup. 'To the Robie House. And not giving up.'

Looking more cautious than enthusiastic, Calder

and Tommy raised their cups, and everyone took a sip.

'Ms Hussey said to leave it alone,' Tommy mumbled.

'That's because she didn't want to see us getting hurt,' Petra said evenly. 'Can you imagine her giving up?'

'No,' Calder said.

'And you think we should?' Petra asked. 'Imagine the thrill of saving one of the greatest houses built in the twentieth century! Why not try?'

'Right,' Tommy said, sitting up straighter.

'Wright!' Petra exclaimed. 'W-R-I-G-H-T. That should be our name: the Wright Three!'

'Cool,' Calder agreed.

Tommy looked uncomfortable as Petra opened her notebook to a blank page and picked up her pencil. He watched as she wrote at the top of the page:

The Wright Three

'So, what now?' Petra asked.

The boys were quiet. Calder pulled out his pentominoes, and Tommy picked a splinter out of his knee.

'How about we share any strange information we know about the house, like stuff we've noticed – things that aren't in books,' Petra suggested.

'How about we don't,' Tommy said rudely.

Petra stared at him.

Calder said, 'Tommy. What's your problem?'

'How do we know our secrets are safe with each other?' Tommy asked.

Petra's eyes widened in irritation and she looked at Calder.

'How about this,' Calder said. 'We need something, some symbol of the Wright Three, that we share every time we think we're getting somewhere. That symbol will mean we trust each other. It could be a sweet or something.'

Tommy brightened. 'I have a big bag of those chewy, red fish at home, the ones that taste great.'

'Perfect!' Petra said. 'Hey – anyone know what a red herring is? Like in a mystery story?'

The boys shook their heads.

'It's a dead-end clue. What if every time we get some good thinking done, we eliminate one of the red herrings?'

Tommy grinned. 'I get it. Eat it!'

'One fish closer to the truth,' Petra nodded.

'Cool,' Calder said.

Petra opened up the notebook again and Tommy's face darkened. 'No writing stuff down,' he said. 'What if someone reads it?'

'She thinks on paper the way I think with pentominoes,' Calder said. 'Let her do it.'

Tommy's chin went up as if he knew it wasn't a good idea.

'How about I make a new code for the notebook, one that's easy to write?' Calder suggested.

'Sounds good,' Petra said. 'And I won't write anything until I have the code. But let's get started – with only eight days until the house comes down, we can't waste time.'

At that moment there was a *tap-scrape-tap* on the glass behind them, and all three jumped. A dead branch whooshed by on the other side of the tree-house window, the grey fingers of twigs bent in a stiff wave.

'I'll start,' Petra said.

She told Calder and Tommy about her visit with Mrs Sharpe, and about the coincidence of hearing the Nantucket ghost story with *The Invisible Man* in it, explaining to Tommy that she'd found two copies of the book last week. She finished with Mrs Sharpe's story of Wright losing a talisman outside the house.

Tommy frowned and chewed on a fingernail.

'That was a lot of secrets,' Calder said, glancing quickly at Tommy. 'OK, I went to visit the mason who fell.'

Now it was Tommy and Petra's turn to stare. Calder then shared what Henry Dare had said about the house shaking him off, and about hearing a voice as he fell. Calder finished by saying he was pretty sure he'd also heard a kid's voice, coming from the house on the day of the demonstration.

'Did either one of you hear something that day?' Calder asked. Tommy and Petra shook their heads. Then Calder talked about the Fibonacci sequence, and noticing it around them in dates, in pentominoes, in what Petra saw in the Robie House windows. He said he was wondering if those numbers were trying to communicate something, something that might help the house.

'Weird,' Petra said.

It was Tommy's turn, but he sat quietly, peeling the plastic off the end of his shoelace. Everything in him wanted to run. If only he had a minute with Goldman, a minute to think. It seemed as though if he'd learned anything in life, he'd learned it was dangerous to trust people. The idea of telling Petra about his find was not only scary, it might be stupid. The stone fish could be the best thing that had ever happened to him.

'Come on, Tommy. I told a bunch of secrets, and Petra did too. Be fair.'

Petra flicked intently at a piece of dirt stuck to her notebook, as if that was more interesting than whatever Tommy was going to say.

'Fine, but if either one of you betrays me, I'll kill you.'

Calder rolled his eyes and waited for Petra to get mad. But when she spoke, her voice was kind. 'No one's going to betray you. Look, you just learned a whole bunch of things from Calder and from me. We're not worried. And you can see I'm not writing anything down. That's because you didn't want me to.'

Tommy swallowed. 'I found a stone fish. A fish in the garden of the Robie House,' he blurted. 'I dug it up, and it looks like it was buried for a long time. I think it's old, and – well, it kind of reminds me of things I've seen in Chinatown.'

Calder grinned and raised his hand in front of his old friend, and Tommy gave him a weak high-five.

'We know Frank Lloyd Wright collected Asian art,' Petra said slowly. 'But Wright collected Japanese prints – what would he have been doing with a small Chinese fish in his pocket?'

'Yeah, I doubt it has anything to do with

Wright,' Tommy added, sucking in his cheeks. 'But I thought the fish might be valuable and that if it was, I'd sell it. My mum and I are saving up for a permanent place to live,' he finished.

'Where is the fish?' Calder asked.

'Goldman has it,' Tommy said.

'Oh!' Petra said. No wonder Tommy had moved the goldfish bowl when she and Calder were there.

Outside the tree-house window, there was a brilliant flash of light followed by the immediate bang and growl of thunder. The sky darkened to a scary black, and the kids started down the ladder, Petra first with her notebook in her mouth.

Partway down, a tremendous gust of wind lifted her shirt. She twisted sideways to cover up. The notebook flew to one side, and she lost sight of it as her hair whipped across her face. Branches were now creaking overhead, and a second flash of lightning was followed by a deafening crash. Big drops of rain began to fall.

The lawn beneath the tree house was overgrown with weeds and bushes, and Petra searched frantically while the boys climbed down.

'My notebook!' she wailed, but the three of them, who hunted until they were soaked, couldn't find it.

Chapter Twenty

AFTER THE STORM

'Oh, no! Goldman! I left the window open.' Tommy spun around and with a quick wave began running for home, splatting straight through the puddles that were already rising on Harper Avenue. He knew he shouldn't be running through the storm with lightning so close, but the thought of Goldman in trouble was too much.

Approaching the Robie House, Tommy remembered the man who had spoken to him on Friday. He stepped out into the empty street so as to be further from the building, and as he ran he looked quickly at the windows.

The rain was pounding down now, and it poured in a smooth sheet from the gutter in front of the French doors on the south side. Through the blur and wobble of running water, he thought he saw a man standing inside. Tommy blinked and stared harder, but kept going. Should he duck back for another look?

No, he said to himself as he stood panting inside the front door of his building. If it was one of the unfriendly work crew, it was better to stay invisible, like the photographer in *Rear Window*, and watch from his lookout.

His jeans were soaked, and it took Tommy a moment to get his apartment key out of his pocket. When he finally slid it into the lock, he found the front door was open.

Funny – either he'd forgotten to lock it this morning, or his mum had come home for lunch and rushed out in a hurry. It had happened before. Tommy turned on the light and closed Goldman's window. His pet's eyes looked frightened and his fins were quivering.

'Poor thing!' Tommy said as he dried the outside of Goldman's bowl. 'You've had quite a week. First a new bowl mate, and then a storm. You're not alone with the treasure, don't worry. We're working on it, the three of us – Petra's in on it too now, and I think she'll be a help. We'll find out what it's worth.'

Goldman had done a terrific job of burying the treasure under his gravel; Tommy couldn't see it at all.

'Good man,' he said soothingly as he changed his clothes.

Then Tommy noticed his fish shelf. All of his treasures were wet and had fallen over, and his glass flounder had lost a fin. He worked carefully for the next fifteen minutes, patting his treasures dry and setting them up again.

As he worked, he had the odd sensation that someone was watching him. He looked towards the dark windows of the Robie House. Without balconies or a big overhang on the north side, rain cascaded down the bricks and glass. The screen on his window was clogged with water, and it was difficult to see clearly.

Even so, he thought now of the photographer in *Rear Window* moving out of the light so as not to be seen from across the way. Tommy backed towards his front door and switched off the overhead bulb. He double-checked the lock as the shadows of the storm collected around him.

Petra gazed miserably out of her front

window. The lightning had stopped, but it was still pouring. Her notebook must be ruined.

She thought now about the way Tommy had dashed off, looking stricken, when he remembered Goldman. He must be a kind person to care so much about his goldfish. She knew he'd lost a bunch of big things – his own dad, a new stepdad, homes that he must have loved. And now he dreamed of selling his latest discovery and helping his mum.

It must be odd, knowing there was no one at home to close the windows. She tried to picture what that might feel like, but couldn't. In all of her twelve and a half years, Petra didn't think she'd ever been home by herself.

When the rain stopped, she headed back towards the Castigliones' garden to look for her notebook.

Calder burst out of his front door. 'I've got something to show you!' he shouted.

'Want to help me find my notebook first?'

Calder nodded, and they ducked into the Castigliones' garden, walking gingerly. Puddles were everywhere, and the flowers and plants were still heavy with water.

Petra spotted a flash of blue in a neighbour's yard and, hurrying over, pulled her notebook from under a giant rhubarb plant. 'I found you!' she crooned under her breath, and patted it dry on her shorts.

Petra and Calder stood on her front porch and opened the notebook. The pages were soaked, and the writing inside had dissolved into a landscape of smears and blots.

She sat down heavily, not even feeling the wet. 'I had a bunch of Tales from the Tracks in here, including one about the man with the cape.'

'Horrible,' Calder agreed, knowing how bad it felt to have his pentominoes scattered. He brightened. 'Hey, what if it's the Invisible Man trying to tell you that visible things can't always stay that way?'

'Mmm,' Petra said slowly, and tried to smile. 'You know what, Calder? This looks like the notebook Mrs Sharpe found under the floorboards on Nantucket, the one she replaced with *The Invisible Man*.'

She wondered if stories and real life were mirroring each other, but in a distorted way. For a moment Petra had the dizzying feeling of looking into a puddle just as a ripple runs across the reflection.

She closed her notebook, and it was then that she saw the scratches – the wind must have flung the book across the top of the chain-link fencing that ran between gardens.

The staggery lines seemed to jump out at her: I M. Now her imagination was *really* going crazy.

She traced them with one finger, and glanced at Calder, who had taken pentominoes out of his pocket and was busily setting them up on a step.

For a second Petra was truly afraid – Mrs Sharpe had been right about *The Invisible Man*. The book put strange ideas into your head. She looked up at the familiar gardens and buildings, and saw a breeze ruffle the bushes by the Castigliones' gate, bending branches and leaves as if someone tall were striding through.

'Hey, Petra. What I wanted to tell you was that just now at home I pulled out three random pieces.

They happened to be the P, the T, and the U or C, whichever way you look at it. That's the three of us! I started playing around with them, and realized I'd made a man – or it was more like the man just appeared.'

Petra saw. The T was upside down on the bottom, the U (or C) was upside down above that, and the P was on top, standing upright.

Calder had made a figure with his head turned, his arms at his sides, his feet going out like a penguin.

'Tommy + Calder + Petra = A Man. But who?' Calder asked, his head on one side.

Sometimes visible and sometimes not ... Mrs Sharpe had tried to tell her that the line between real and unreal was sometimes hard to find. And now Calder had said the same thing.

Petra looked directly at him. 'Maybe it's the Invisible Man.'

'Maybe,' Calder said casually as he knocked the man over and loaded the pieces into his pocket, but Petra saw him glance quickly over his shoulder.

'Remember, don't start a new notebook until I

make you a code,' he added in a loud voice, as if to be sure that everyone heard.

Petra nodded, and watched him hop down the porch steps two at a time, look in both directions, and head towards home. She sat for several more minutes, following the clouds overhead and enjoying the cool air pulled in by the storm. Then, in the mud next to the kerb, she saw footsteps.

The heavy prints of a man with bare feet ran between and then beneath two parked cars. She was sure they hadn't been there a moment before.

Chapter Twenty-one

A NEW CODE

The next morning was already steamy and hot by ten o'clock.

'So here it is. Complete privacy,' Calder said proudly, tapping the new notebook. He, Tommy and Petra were sitting in the Medici Bakery, a special treat funded by Calder's mum.

'I've written two sentences here, and you don't need any table to decode this. The message is right in front of you if you can see it.'

Petra and Tommy looked at Calder's block letters:

P'TUHW'INST T'IMSU U'TNOP
IKNEYEM'PI FAZ'NI'YLOU'NYEP
W'FYRTOW'ML NRZETANDP'II'NNGY
V'WLHUAP'TU T'IM T'WIRN'IZ'TUEN -
UJF'UNSI'TY M'IF'NU UCTAMSTEP!

'I've called it the Wright Sandwich Code,' Calder said. 'That's a hint.'

'Whoa,' Petra muttered, and then moved her lips silently for a moment.

Tommy leaned over the table, his eyes skating back and forth over the jumble of letters. 'Anything to do with pentominoes being the bread?' he asked.

'Yup,' Calder said, grinning. 'So can you read it?'

Petra looked up.

'I've got the pentominoes, but the punctuation thing ...' Tommy whispered to himself.

Petra had never seen Tommy when he wasn't looking either distracted or self-conscious. His entire body was focused now, hunched intently over the piece of paper.

She stopped trying and watched him, fascinated. Suddenly he grabbed the pencil and wrote:

IGTRZETAN'TY Z'INDUEXAM

Calder reached across the table and whacked Tommy, and Tommy punched him back.

'So?' Petra said. 'Explain.'

Tommy did, and Calder thought he'd never felt so happy. Seeing Tommy's round, shiny head next to Petra's curly black one, the two of them talking excitedly, made Calder want to jump up and down.

Petra then wrote:

M'PIETRN'FXELCM'TU!

'If you didn't know what pentominoes were, you'd never get this,' Petra said admiringly. 'And it's still not easy,' she added.

'Not so hard,' Tommy beamed at her. 'I'm a finder. But why both the W and the M letters?' he asked Calder.

His old friend shrugged. 'W for Wright. M for the Invisible Man. And I wanted thirteen.'

'Every other letter counts, and the apostrophe just marks the letters that are a part of the message but also happen to be pentominoes,' Petra said. 'Very tricky.'

Just then the door to the bakery opened, and two familiar faces came into view. Tommy flipped the notebook shut.

'Ms Hussey!' Petra said. Their teacher was wearing shorts and an orange tank top, and her hair was tied back with a crinkly yellow ribbon.

'Mr Dare!' Calder said, and looked from one to the other. Mr Dare was walking with a limp, but without his cane. He'd had a haircut, and looked much better than he had in the hospital – he wasn't quite as red.

'So how's the first day of the holidays?' Ms Hussey asked.

'Good,' the Wright Three said in one voice.

As if she could read the question in their minds, she added, 'Mr Dare and I met the day of the demonstration.' She blinked rapidly, as if she'd said too much.

Mr Dare cleared his throat. 'You kids did a good job with the press. Yes, he's the one who came to see me,' the mason said, and looked evenly at Calder. 'I told him about my fall.'

'And I spoke with Mrs Sharpe after you did, Petra,' Ms Hussey said, as if this explained things. 'Well, glad to see you all together.' Ms Hussey smiled, and now it was the kids' turn to look embarrassed.

Mr Dare ordered two coffees to go, and didn't

ask Ms Hussey what she wanted in hers. How long had they known each other, Petra wondered. How did he know she wanted cream and four sugars? And what did Mrs Sharpe tell her that fitted with something Mr Dare had told Calder?

Calder wondered how much Henry Dare had told Ms Hussey about their conversation. Tommy wondered why Ms Hussey had made that remark about the three of them. Petra was still wondering why their teacher and the mason were together.

When Mr Dare came back to the table, he put the two coffees down for a moment. He looked at the change in his palm, a quarter, a dime and a penny. 'See these?' he asked. 'They're going to disappear.' He shifted the change from one hand to the other, and suddenly both palms were empty. 'See? Gone.' He even held his hands up in the air. 'Now. I might need that change later.' Suddenly he reached behind Petra's ear and pulled out the quarter. Then he pulled the dime off Tommy's sleeve and the penny from the pocket of Calder's T-shirt. He showed them the change, then slipped it into his pocket. 'Now you see it, now you don't,' he beamed.

'Well, happy beginning of summer,' Ms Hussey said. Mr Dare waved as the door to the bakery closed behind them.

'He's pretty clever,' Tommy said.

'Maybe too clever,' Calder said, peering out.

'Ms Hussey's looking at her watch,' Petra said. 'Maybe they're getting on the train.'

Tommy was on his feet. 'Come on! Let's see where they're going.'

Walking along 57th Street, Ms Hussey looked relaxed, and Mr Dare looked at Ms Hussey. The three kids ducked in and out of doorways and peered from behind parked cars. All three felt foolish. Hiding in broad daylight wasn't easy. They agreed that if they were spotted, they'd explain they were on their way to Powell's.

Ms Hussey and Mr Dare leaned over the giveaway box outside the bookshop, picking up first one book and then another. Then all the books went back, and they turned down Harper Avenue, walking purposefully towards 59th Street.

They were talking and laughing, and Ms Hussey

was gesticulating. The kids walked silently on the far side of the street, trying to look as if they were just enjoying the morning.

When they reached the train underpass at the end of the block, Ms Hussey and Mr Dare were gone.

'They must be up on the platform,' Calder said. All three knew that they weren't allowed to go downtown without asking, but this was clearly a special situation.

'How do we know this guy isn't just pretending to be friendly? What if Ms Hussey's in danger?' Tommy thought of the worker outside the Robie House the morning after the demonstration.

'Yeah, what if he's luring her somewhere? Maybe he's afraid she'll stir up more trouble,' Petra dug in her pocket. 'Great – I still have some grocery money. I'll explain to my mum later.'

They hurried across Harper Avenue, waited beneath the underpass until the train roared in overhead, then flew up the stairs and down the platform to the nearest door. Once in the train carriage, they were relieved not to see either adult. Tommy pulled a sandwich bag of red fish out of his pocket, and passed it around.

'Red herring time,' he said. They each ate one.

At the Van Buren stop, where they'd got off on their class trip to the Art Institute earlier that year, they spotted a flash of orange whisking into a stairwell. But by the time they were out of their seats and off the train, there was no sign of their teacher or the mason. Tommy's eyes skated along the carriages behind theirs, and he saw a set of heavy black glasses very like the ones on the man outside the Robie House, the man who had frightened him.

'Hey!' Tommy said, and at that moment the man raised his newspaper so nothing was visible but the top of his baseball cap.

'It's that man I saw by the Robie House!' Tommy said, but by the time his words were out, the train had whooshed by. 'I think,' he finished lamely, then told Calder and Petra about what had happened several days ago on the way to school.

'Spies must have a hard time not imagining

things,' Petra agreed. 'Once you get suspicious, everything looks important.'

The three formed a tidy equilateral triangle on the platform, the crowd parting around them. 'Well, how about we go to the Art Institute?' Calder said. 'Knowing Ms Hussey, if she's not being kidnapped she's probably taking Mr Dare to the museum.'

Petra added, 'And if they're not there, we could check for something similar to your fish, Tommy.'

'Good idea,' Tommy said. 'If we find something like it, I could bring the fish in and show it to one of the museum people.'

'Yeah – tell them a family member gave it to you,' Calder said. 'And if it's worth a bundle, maybe they'll buy it!'

The three walked along Michigan Avenue towards the Art Institute, but saw no sign of Ms Hussey and Mr Dare. The midday sun glinted mercilessly off skyscraper windows, off cars creeping through traffic, off the pavement beneath their feet. It was a relief to enter the museum.

'Hey – Chinese, Japanese and Korean Art,' Calder read aloud. They stood in front of an invitingly dim doorway on the first floor. 'Let's check it out.'

Petra and Tommy joined him in front of a statue of a muscular man wearing nothing but shorts and a piece of cloth tied around his waist. His hair stood straight up on his head, he was frowning hideously, and he had three glass eyes, one in the middle of his forehead. In his right hand he clutched what looked like a heavy stick. The veins on his arm stood out with the effort.

'Awesome,' Calder said.

'Japanese Thunderbolt Deity,' Petra read, squinting at the shadowy wall label. 'Twelfth century. It says here that the thunderbolt represents the power of wisdom to penetrate ignorance and destroy evil.'

There were four other guardian statues in the room, each in a separate glass case. One, grimacing horribly, had close-together eyes, fangs, fat cheeks, and what looked like a wig of curly hair. 'Japanese: one of the five Buddhist Lords of

Light,' Petra read. 'He represents wrath against evil. Hey, just like the Wright Three.' She turned to look at Tommy and Calder, who were busy making hideous faces at each other.

Just then they heard a familiar voice, faint but unmistakable. 'A mystery?' Ms Hussey asked.

Chapter Twenty-two

WRIGHT'S FISH

'Hide!'

Calder ducked to the left, into a room filled with large ceramic statues, Tommy ran to the right and Petra straight ahead.

Calder's room was alive with a parade of large horses, camels, and musclemen stepping on what looked like angry gnomes, all displayed in floor-to-ceiling glass cases. He dropped to a crouch and slid sideways into an alcove. A wall label above his head read: Buddhist Pagoda, 724 AD. He added the numbers in the date and got thirteen.

'Garden Statues Trampling Demons!' Ms Hussey exclaimed.

'I want one,' Mr Dare said.

Calder could just see them on the far side of the room, facing in his direction. Had they spotted him?

On the far side of a wooden screen Petra

found a dark corner and sank to a sitting position, hugging her knees. She could see the calm profile of an elegant seated woman, a statue as big as she was. She had two extra arms on her right side, and all three arms waved in different directions.

'A secret ...' she heard Mr Dare's voice coming from another room, but which one? There was an opening behind her, a door diagonally ahead, and another two or three doors visible in the next room. The place was perfect for a game of hide and seek.

Next she saw Ms Hussey's orange shirt move slowly through a room with many pale-green vases and bowls.

'Tragedies in that house ... celery ...' her teacher said as she bent to look at a round pot with a bird's head on the top. Celery? What on earth were they talking about? As Ms Hussey and Mr Dare's voices faded into the next room, Petra took a deep breath and looked around. Tommy and Calder were nowhere in sight.

⊞⊞⊞ Tommy had found himself in a long gallery with framed prints on the wall. He knelt behind a display case. Inside was one of the largest teapots he'd ever seen, a delicious tangerine red with a black handle. It was just the kind of thing his mum would love.

The prints were detailed landscapes filled with people doing cheerful things: walking over bridges, chatting, hanging clothes. A piece of writing on the wall explained that they were by a Japanese artist named Hokusai, and mentioned Frank Lloyd Wright as an adviser to the man who'd collected them. Wow – Wright got around.

Tommy waited in deep silence for what felt like a long time. No one entered or even passed by the room, not even a guard. Where was everyone? Through a far doorway, he could see a larger-than-life green Buddha seated on a throne.

The room was airy and square, divided by low glass cases containing a sprinkling of brightly coloured ornaments. Tommy took two steps towards the Buddha, then heard voices and the sound of Ms Hussey laughing. He spun round, ran towards a set of darkened glass doors that said Please Enter and darted inside.

He was in a forest of black columns. An exhibit of painted screens glowed at the far end of the room. To the right, behind glass, was a row of gigantic vases – some were big enough for a small kid to hide in. Finding himself alone in the room, he breathed a sigh of relief. It was then that he saw Ms Hussey reach for the door handle.

Tommy hurried towards a corner, hoping to press against the wall and not be seen. There, running parallel to the room, was a passageway that led towards a door that said 'Staff Only'. What luck!

'Amazing space,' Ms Hussey exclaimed. 'Peaceful ...'

'Looks like a cave,' Mr Dare said. 'Nothing in here that's small enough. Let's keep going.'

Nothing small enough ... So they were hunting too. Tommy's eyes grew big. He counted to ten and popped out of his hiding place. Ms Hussey and Mr Dare had left the adjoining room and were headed through another. Tommy ran quietly after them, ducking behind a family with four kids. He was just congratulating himself on his expert spying when he stubbed his toe on the corner of a display case.

'Ow!' he whispered, and kicked the case with

his other foot. Ms Hussey turned at the sound, and Tommy crumpled awkwardly to the floor and rolled out of sight. The family moved on. As he checked for blood, something poked him in the back.

Calder was crouching beside him, and Petra was behind Calder.

'You OK?' Petra whispered, trying not to laugh.

Tommy scowled. 'Fine,' he whispered back, although his toe was killing him.

Calder got up on his knees and peeked through the glass. He gave the thumbs-up sign. 'They're gone.'

'Mr Dare said they're looking for something small – come on!' Tommy said, and the three crept in single file, Tommy limping after Calder, into a room filled with blue and white china. They were surrounded by painted fish and dragons.

Tommy's heart began to pound.

The room ended in a hall with freestanding cases running down the middle. The kids spotted their teacher and the mason in front of a wall display, and tiptoed along behind them, hiding just out of sight behind three gigantic bells. Suddenly they didn't care if they were caught – they needed to try to find out what Mr Dare knew, and whether Ms Hussey was safe.

'You remember my great-grandfather was Frank Lloyd Wright's mason,' Mr Dare said. 'Well, Wright went to Japan shortly before he built the Robie House.'

'Yes, 1905,' Ms Hussey murmured.

'Oh,' Mr Dare sounded surprised. 'Done some research, have you?'

'A bit,' Ms Hussey said cautiously.

'Well, here's a secret you won't find in any book: Wright apparently bought a little present for himself in Japan – a very old jade fish that had been made in China. Who knows – maybe it was exactly like the carvings here. It was his talisman, a good-luck piece that he carried in his pocket.

'The Japanese inherited many of their tales from China, and Wright had apparently heard an ancient Chinese legend about a carp that swims upriver and leaps over waterfalls and becomes a dragon, which was a desirable thing. Asian dragons symbolize wisdom and the power to rule. The Emperor, for instance, always had dragons embroidered on his clothing. Ambitious fellow, that Wright.

'Well, according to my great-grandfather, Wright carried this talisman for two or three years. And then one day during the construction of the Robie House, the fish fell through a hole in Wright's pocket. He was sure it had happened on the south side of the house, where workers were digging a trench. He was very upset and told all of the men, even offered a reward. As far as I know the carp was never found.'

Tommy, his mind whirling, couldn't look at Calder and Petra. *I have Frank Lloyd Wright's fish! I found it, I found it!*

Petra remembered Mrs Sharpe's story about the lost talisman and her hint about a mystery attached to the house.

Calder tried not to think – he could already smell trouble.

'Wow,' Ms Hussey said. 'That's a great story.'

Mr Dare continued, 'And that's not all. After the house was finished, Wright confided in my great-grandfather that since the carp would have to remain at the site, and it symbolized his own passage from carp to dragon at a difficult time in his life, he had coded himself into the structure. The idea was that a part of him would remain behind at the house with his talisman – so that his voyage could continue. He laughed about it being a superstitious thing to do, but my great-grandfather could tell it was no joke.'

'Fabulous!' Ms Hussey's voice sounded strange – either excited or afraid. 'And where is the code?'

'Apparently Wright never told anyone. He talked about leaving an invisible man or something behind, but that was it. During my couple of days in the house, I kept an eye out for initials, a hidden compartment, a buried piece of paper or a photograph, but I never found anything.'

The Wright Three were hardly breathing.

Ms Hussey spoke, her voice now bright and eager. 'But he made it! He built Fallingwater! That's a brilliant house that Wright built in Pennsylvania twenty-five years after the Robie House, a house that sits on the crest of a waterfall. Hey, he made it to the top of the falls, he *did* become a dragon, so his fish talisman must have worked! Maybe that's why he had to save the Robie House, and save it twice ...'

There were a series of rustling noises as the two headed for the exit. Quiet resettled on the Asian wing.

Tommy took a long, deep breath – he felt dizzy. Calder and Petra were already on their feet and pulling him over towards the wall case.

In front of them was an array of small, stone fish. All were curved, like Tommy's, and one had a dragony head. A number had the same finely etched spiral pattern on them. All were about the same size as Tommy's find, maybe five centimetres long, and all were jade.

Calder whacked his old friend on the back. 'It's the discovery of a lifetime, Tommy! You found something so ancient – you'll go into the Hall of Fame for Finders!'

Tommy grinned. If anything, the carving he had found was an exquisitely detailed version of the creatures in front of them. In comparison to these other fish, his find was a small masterpiece.

'It's a wish come true,' Petra added, peering eagerly at the wall label. 'Chinese, Eastern Zhou Dynasty, about fourth to sixth century BC.' She turned towards Calder and Tommy, her eyes shining. 'BC! That's more than 2,000 years old!'

'It must be worth a ton!' Calder exclaimed. 'At least one house, maybe two. You and your mum can buy any place you want in Hyde Park now.'

Petra winced as if she'd been stung. 'What're you saying? Selling Wright's fish is what will save the Robie House – that must be why we found it. Tommy can't sell it and keep the money! We just made a discovery that will save one of the greatest pieces of art ever built.'

'We? We? I found that fish,' Tommy blurted, finding his voice. 'And it's mine.' Suddenly he realized he was trapped, horribly trapped – everything he'd always wanted was in plain sight, and yet now he might not get it. Was he going to lose the best find he'd ever made, a find that might make up for all the other things he'd lost? To his horror, he felt his eyes fill with tears.

Why had he ever joined the Wright Three?

Petra turned away while Tommy wiped his face on his T-shirt. Calder said gently, 'That's OK. I'd be whacko too. It's hard to believe, isn't it?'

ꟷ ꟷ ꟷ The ride home on the train was silent. It was Calder who suggested they each have some thinking time on the way back to Hyde Park and then talk things over in the tree house. They sat several seats apart, forming an awkward scalene triangle. No one mentioned the red herrings.

Tommy tried to feel happy about what he'd suspected all along – the carving was very, very valuable. He had uncovered something extraordinary, something that others had tried hard to find.

And he knew Petra was right – selling the fish to a museum would probably mean the Robie House could be saved. The art in museums was always worth millions, wasn't it? This was a kind of miracle. He could prevent the murder of a great work of art, something an entire university had been unable to do. He wanted to save the house, yes. But did Petra understand what a real home meant? He

didn't think so.

And what about his mum? In his head, he could hear her telling him to put the money towards saving the Wright house. Family, she always said, was about being together, not about owning things or living in a specific place. Tommy wasn't sure this was the whole truth – of course she'd love to have her own home. He knew those lines in her forehead when it was time to move again, and she always sighed at the sight of boxes and packing tape.

What would Mr Wright tell him to do?

Tommy thought he and Mr Wright would like each other, even though dads who disappeared were not Tommy's favourite kind. Wright was tough in a good way – even at the worst moments in his life, he had never given up. Ms Hussey had shared stories with the class about Wright's three marriages, and also some tragic things that had happened to him, things that were not his fault. Four years after the Robie House was finished, a woman Wright had loved very much was brutally murdered, with her two young children, in the house he built for her. He was away on business, and it was an ugly, freakish happening. Then there had been times when Wright had no work or money, and seemed entirely forgotten by the world. He had been called selfish and stubborn, but even when he wasn't popular he had stuck to what he believed in.

Tommy thought to himself that both he and Frank Lloyd Wright knew about determination, about getting where you needed to go. Tommy felt quite sure that the great man would want him to keep and sell the fish, and in doing so continue on his own journey to becoming a dragon, a highly successful finder – a finder who earned a home for himself and his family. The dragon-fish had worked for Wright, and now it would work for Tommy.

And then he had a sneaky idea. What if no one but the Wright Three knew where Tommy had found the fish? He could pretend he'd found it in the Japanese Garden, which was a ten-minute walk from Harper Avenue. The garden was a part of a small island where Tommy and Calder had often dug for treasures, a place where Japanese master-craftsmen had built an amazing temple more than a hundred years ago during a World's Fair that took place in Chicago. Although the building was gone now, the garden was still there. Millions of people had come to Hyde Park for that fair. Someone could easily have dropped the jade fish on that piece of land.

And, after all, Wright had kept many secrets during his lifetime. Maybe great men couldn't reveal all their secrets, at least not instantly.

But would Petra and Calder agree not to tell where Tommy had really found the fish?

And then Tommy had an even better idea.

Chapter Twenty-three

A LIE

Looking out of the train window, Petra thought about the strange and magical side of what had happened in the last week.

Was it just luck that Tommy had dug up a priceless jade fish right when it was needed, after it had been in the ground for almost a century?

And was it just coincidence that she had found the two Invisible Man books, and that Wright had talked about leaving an invisible man of some kind in the Robie House?

She had stuck one of the copies of *The Invisible Man* in her jacket pocket that morning, meaning to show it to Tommy now that they were the Wright Three. She pulled it out now, and closing her eyes flipped back and forth through the pages and put her finger down.

She opened her eyes and read:

All men, however highly educated, retain some superstitious inklings.

Who was superstitious? Frank Lloyd Wright? Was she? What was the book telling her?

And was it superstitious to think coincidences weren't just coincidences?

Calder was thinking codes.

Wright had left a code of some kind in the house, and he'd also mentioned an invisible man. The house was a puzzle, Calder sensed that was true, a puzzle that couldn't be broken into pieces without destroying its meaning, just like a set of pentominoes.

As a kid, Wright had played with a set of maths tools called Froebel blocks. Ms Hussey had talked about them and brought in pictures. Some of the blocks resembled pentominoes. Wright claimed that moving those blocks around as a child had changed the way he thought, and helped make him the architect he was. And Wright had written that he always loved making up the language in his famous stained glass windows.

Calder admired the matter-of-fact way Wright said that, and remembered it – he'd even asked Ms

Hussey a few days ago if he could try writing with shapes and not words, and she'd said yes, as long as he was communicating. He'd enthusiastically made rows and columns of triangles, quadrilaterals, pentagons and hexagons, but that was as far as he'd got. The idea was better than the reality.

Could Wright's code be made up of repeating shapes? Could a certain number and order of geometrical forms equal certain letters in the alphabet? Or could the code be imprinted in some way in the brickwork?

How about Wright leaving an invisible man behind – Calder knew Petra must be thinking about this too.

And Tommy – Calder knew he was thinking about the opposite, about becoming a very visible kid who lived in his own, visible home.

None of the three looked forward to the meeting in the tree house.

They climbed the ladder silently, Tommy first and Petra last. Tommy pulled out the bag of red fish and dropped it on the tree-house floor.

'Red herring time!' Calder tried to say cheerfully. They each took one, but no one smiled.

Petra leaned back against a wall and opened her notebook. It was quiet except for the tapping sounds of Calder's pentominoes, the occasional murmur of mourning doves and the whisper of leaves. They hardly noticed an occasional twig-snap coming from the branch that reached over the tracks.

Tommy cleared his throat. 'I lied,' he said, sucking in his cheeks.

Calder and Petra stared at him.

'I told Calder I'd found the fish in the Robie House garden because I was thinking about telling the class. I wanted kids to notice me, and to think I'd done something brave. I didn't find it there, and that means it isn't Wright's fish.'

'So where did it come from?' Calder asked, trying to hide his shock. He didn't remember Tommy ever lying about anything – not to his oldest friend. This wasn't good.

'The Japanese Garden,' Tommy said, and bit hard on his thumbnail.

'*What?*' Petra said. 'Why didn't you tell us sooner?'

Tommy shrugged. 'I didn't think it really made a difference.'

Petra had a dark-red spot in each cheek. She looked like *she* was going to cry. This was one weird day, Calder thought to himself.

Closing the notebook, Petra said, 'But you can still save the Robie House with that fish, even though it wasn't Wright's. It's still worth a lot of money, maybe a fortune – you can be a hero! And we'll never breathe a word about your first story.'

'I don't think that's what Wright would want me to do,' Tommy muttered.

'What do you mean?' Petra's voice was getting squeaky. 'He cared more about that house than any other house he ever built – he saved it twice, twice, once right before he died, and now we can save it the third time – the Wright Three, that's us!'

'But ...' Calder was stirring his pentominoes on the tree-house floor. 'Maybe, if Ms Hussey was right, he saved the house because of the carp-dragon story, because of losing his talisman, and not so much for the house itself. And once he got there, once he became a dragon … No, never mind. He kept saving it even when he was super-famous, didn't he?'

'It was the house!' Petra practically shrieked. 'Of course it was the house! And you want to sell the fish, keep the money, live in some fancy place and let the Robie House be murdered?'

She turned towards Tommy, facing him directly. 'You're … you're … despicable,' she finished.

Tommy crossed his arms and stuck out his lower lip. 'And *you* don't know what it's like to never have your own house, to only have a mum and a goldfish in your family, and to lose two dads.' Tommy's voice wavered on the 'two'.

He went on, 'Wright is dead. I'm alive. Is some old house more important than my family?'

Petra looked at Tommy with a kinder expression. 'No,' she said slowly.

'I get it that you want your own home, you've had a bunch of tough moves, but … You think your mum would let you keep the money from this fish?' Calder asked.

'What if it didn't occur to her that the money could save the Robie House?' Tommy asked. 'After all, it's only a coincidence, us hearing this talisman story about Wright and me finding the fish at the same time.'

'But won't you feel bad about hiding something so important?' Petra asked. 'Won't you feel guilty when the first chainsaw bites into the Robie House and you have to watch out of your window, knowing you could have saved it?'

All three were silent, picturing the twinkly glass in the windows and the inviting, maze-like look of the house.

Tommy covered his forehead with the palms of both hands. 'Let me think about it,' he said.

Ten minutes later, Tommy put the key into his door. When he turned it, he found it was already unlocked.

He knew his mum wouldn't be home for another hour, and he realized now that he'd forgotten to tell her about finding the door unlocked yesterday. It was a good thing Hyde Park was such a safe neighbourhood.

When he opened the door this time, his heart practically stopped.

Chapter Twenty-four

HORROR

The apartment was a nightmare. Clothes were thrown everywhere, broken dishes were scattered across the floor, and the window sill was empty.

Goldman! Tommy dashed across the room, crunching on glass, and gasped with horror. The pondweed and gravel were everywhere, but where was Goldman? Tommy got down on his hands and knees.

His pet lay gasping in several centimetres of water, miraculously cradled in a corner of the fish bowl that had flown under his bed. Tommy, shaking now, carefully pulled the fragment of glass towards himself, and Goldman flopped out of this tiny bit of water in a panic. Tommy tried to put him back in, but Goldman was too upset to stay still.

Tommy raced to the kitchen, grabbed a plastic food container, sloshed bottled water into it, and raced back. He felt a piece of glass sink deep into

one knee as he knelt back down and lifted Goldman tenderly into the container.

At first his pet floated to the surface, on his side. 'Oh, Goldman! Please! You can do it! You're tough,' Tommy whispered.

If Goldman died, he knew a part of him would die too.

Suddenly Goldman righted himself and took a quick dive around the container, as if checking it out. Tommy whooped for joy.

He took the largest mixing bowl he could find, filled it with the rest of the bottled water, and carefully transferred Goldman. The bowl was empty, which wasn't much fun for his pet ...

The bowl was empty!

Tommy searched frantically through the mess on the floor. He pawed through the wet remains of his fish collection, and looked under pillows and around open books. By now the blood was running freely down his leg, but he didn't even notice. Could the fish have slid under the bed? No ... Fallen between two pieces of china? No ... It was true: his find, the find of a lifetime, was gone.

Someone had known he had it. Someone had come looking for it – who could that be?

Not Calder or Petra ... And the idea of Ms Hussey wrecking his apartment to find the fish was crazy. But Mr Dare ...

He had quit the crew, because of his fall, but was he still friends with them? Had he told them the story of Wright's talisman? Tommy thought of the guy with the black glasses.

And then Tommy had a creepy thought: only someone standing on the south side of the Robie House could have seen him scraping the dirt off his find, jumping up from the garden, and racing back to his apartment.

Just then he heard the squeak-click of the door knob turning, and realized it was too late to do anything but grab for a weapon. He picked up a large, deadly crescent of glass.

Chapter Twenty-five

IN THE BOXES

Zelda Segovia's face appeared in the doorway, her mouth opening in a slow O. Tommy had never, ever been so glad to see anyone.

He rushed over and gave her a giant hug.

'What happened? Are you OK?' his mum asked, dropping her bag of groceries on the floor and adding a broken bottle of milk to the mess.

'B-break-in!' Tommy stuttered, the words catching in his mouth.

They stood in the puddle of milk while she held Tommy close. 'Oh, thank God you weren't hurt! None of this matters – I'm just so thankful you're in one piece.'

Tommy felt a painful twinge when his mum said, 'none of this matters'. He didn't know how to tell her about the missing jade fish, not when he'd kept it a secret for so many days. He needed time to think, he had to think ... One thing he did know: he had to tell Calder and Petra, and tell them right away.

He overheard his mum telling a police officer that nothing of value was missing – it was sickening hearing her say that, but of course it wasn't her fault. While she spoke with two detectives who were dusting the apartment for fingerprints, Tommy went into the kitchen, pretended to be talking to Goldman, and quietly phoned Calder. He whispered the news.

Calder kept saying, '*What?*' and sounded just as dazed as Tommy felt.

'Call Petra,' Tommy said, and hung up.

After the cut on Tommy's knee was cleaned and bandaged, the locksmith came to change the lock and add a heavy bolt to the inside of the door.

Tommy and his mum picked up the broken china and washed the floor. That afternoon they went to the petshop and bought Goldman a new bowl, a perfect sphere the pale-green colour of sea glass.

'This is nicer than your old home,' Tommy told him as Goldman explored. The gravel on the bottom was multi-coloured this time, and Tommy anchored a fresh bunch of pondweed by a red footbridge he'd bought. Just for safety, he put a tiny onyx shark, one from his collection that hadn't been smashed, on the bridge. Now Goldman had a guard.

After Goldman was settled in, Tommy's mum stood in the kitchen with her hands on her hips, looking at the empty cupboard. Every plate and glass had been smashed.

'Good thing I save jars,' she said cheerfully. 'And good thing we haven't taken all our boxes down to the basement storage room yet.' With Tommy's help, she pulled box after box out of the wardrobe in her bedroom, and they made a pile of mis-matched dishes.

'It's good to see these again,' Tommy said. 'They're so familiar.'

'I know, you never did like change. Mr Keep-Everything, that's you,' his mum said fondly.

Tommy was looking at favourite baby toys and some of his old board books. Then he pulled out something unfamiliar: a plastic box with two receivers next to it.

'Hey, what's this?'

His mum laughed. 'Your old baby monitor. Your

OLD TOYS
etc.

dad and I were living in a gigantic house at the time you were born. The monitor goes in the baby's room, then the parent keeps the receiver, and even the tiniest sounds can be heard – quite amazing, really. I never could bring myself to get rid of that stuff, especially after your dad was gone.'

There was a short silence.

'He would be so proud of the fact that you're a finder. It's a shame so much of your fish collection was destroyed today.'

'Mmm,' Tommy nodded. 'But I won't give up.'

'That's my guy,' his mum said, rubbing his back.

'Can I have this?' Tommy asked, holding up the baby monitor.

'Sure,' his mum said, closing the boxes again. 'Come on. Let's put these in the kitchen and go out to dinner. We need a treat. How about Chinatown?'

Chapter Twenty-six

A SILVERY VOICE

Calder phoned late that afternoon. Petra had just written in the notebook:

W'WNET LAPRIEZ UST'UNRVEX I'FL'INSLHU
P'INSI P'VTAP'LT'UTANBI'LIEU. X'WIHMYU
F'WIETRIEZ I'MPSMHI'UTSUSTEX'YT
NAN'NIDV U'MTRIDRAXRIET P'IN'NI
TAFSV'ILAP'NY T'WN'IN'NIGY?
TSUOP'MVEN'TIHM'I Z'NUGP UWTRLONTGZ.

She sat quietly now, trying to absorb the terrible news about the break-in. She and Calder had agreed that it all seemed too mean: the near death of Goldman, the destruction of most of Tommy's fish collection, and then the theft of what Tommy had just learned was truly the find of a lifetime. Never mind the thought that Tommy would probably have changed his mind, done the right thing, and sold the fish in order to save the Robie House.

A nightmare, that's what this was. They had been so close to rescuing the house, and now something creepy and ugly had happened. Had the criminal broken in to steal the fish, or had he grabbed the fish not knowing what it was?

Tommy told Calder that he and Petra shouldn't tell their parents about the jade carving, not yet. He wanted his mum to be the first to know. Besides, Tommy had said to Calder on the phone, the Wright Three needed to decide what to do.

Petra liked the sound of that. But ... could they get the fish back themselves? It was a scary idea.

Her bed wasn't far from her window and she looked out now, breathing in the lavender light. Ordinarily she loved this time of day at this time of year – the combination of crickets and tree frogs, a quiet sky, and the way shadows melted into the lush bloom of darkness behind houses and under trees. Storybook evenings.

But not tonight.

Something was wrong with this whole picture, very wrong. Petra could feel it. For one thing, there were too many coincidences.

She tried to separate them out, but couldn't. She decided to write. Abandoning the code, she sat with her back against the wall and a tall pillow on either side of her. There: no IM could read over her shoulder now, and too bad if anyone else found the notebook.

1. The Invisible Man: I found him, he feels real. Mrs Sharpe mentioned the book. Who is Wright's invisible man?

2. The Threes: the house seemed to be telling me three at the same time Calder was building with three pentominoes. Calder picked F and L and W out of his pentominoes again and again ... and the C and P and T pieces made the figure of a man. There is a man somewhere. But how can he be invisible?

3. The Fish: why did Tommy find a fish just like Frank Lloyd Wright's

talisman, but in the Japanese Garden? It's a likely spot, but how could it have happened at just the right moment for the Robie House? Chance?

4. The Art Institute: why did Mr Dare take Ms Hussey to look for small Asian art objects and tell her that story? Does he know Tommy found something? Does she?

For once, writing didn't seem to help. If only the house itself could talk ... It could tell the kids who had broken into Tommy's apartment next door. It could tell them what Wright would have wanted Tommy to do with that jade fish. It could tell them what to do.

Petra closed her eyes and pictured the house sitting through almost a century of lavender evenings ... through the green light of thunderstorms ... through snows piled high on the ledges and balconies ... through three families who loved it, and three families who laughed and also cried ...

What would you like us to do? She asked the house silently.

A thin, silvery voice filled Petra's mind:

This house is me, it's mine, and if it is torn apart I will be too. I am one with the brick and wood and glass and light. I am sad, joyful, dangerous, playful, powerful and fragile. If you trust me enough to listen to my message, I will speak.

Was she making this up? No, she wasn't! *I'm listening*, she sent back. *I'm listening!*

But there was only silence. Petra opened her eyes.

What had just happened? Maybe it didn't matter if she understood. She now felt sure of one thing, sure to the very bottom of her heart: There was something alive in that building.

Chapter Twenty-seven

A TRIANGLE OF GOLD

Sitting in Moon Palace, Tommy and his mum watched three giant carp swimming in a tank the size of a bathtub by the front door. His mum had been right: it was a relief to get away from home tonight.

'I wonder how big Goldman will get,' Tommy mused.

'Are you going to have a carp pool when you're rich and famous?' his mum asked with a smile.

'Absolutely,' Tommy answered.

Then they talked about day trips they might want to take that summer, about going to look at some of the other houses Frank Lloyd Wright had built in Chicago, and about movies to rent. After egg rolls, orange chicken, broccoli and peapods, Tommy cracked open his fortune cookie. He read:

Don't give up. In darkness, much work can be accomplished.

What? He stuffed the fortune deep in his pocket. 'What's yours, Mum?' he asked, seeing his mother frown as she chewed her cookie.

'Something about watch out for neighbours who use their blinds,' she said.

'No blinds in the Robie House,' Tommy said quickly. 'Only in *Rear Window*.'

'Right.' His mum patted his shoulder.

When they left the restaurant, Tommy watched with horror as the man with black glasses stepped into an antiques shop across the street.

First Tommy had seen him on the train this morning and now here? Was this guy following him? He remembered his threatening words: *I wouldn't feel so proud if I were you.* Could he have been the one who broke into their apartment? Did he have Tommy's fish?

Tommy dragged his mum back into Moon Palace, and peered out of the front of the restaurant through the drinking fountain.

'What on earth—' she said.

'It's a man who works at the Robie House. He doesn't like me, and I think he's up to something.'

'What?' Zelda Segovia asked, her voice now tight and anxious. 'What is this about?'

'Well – I think that guy is trying to scare us kids away from saving the Robie House. Remember there was all the newspaper stuff about our demonstration, and a group of important people are visiting soon, including the mayor. This worker probably wants to be sure we don't pop up again and make trouble.' Tommy's mind was going a mile a minute. 'Maybe that's who wrecked our apartment, thinking he could make us move out. After all, Goldman and I have a Number One lookout.'

'That you do,' his mum said slowly. 'But why should he be scared of a bunch of kids? And why do something so terrible to us?'

'Well ...' Tommy said again.

'Have you been poking around the Robie House?' his mum asked.

'Not really,' Tommy said, and sucked in his cheeks.

'Tommy Segovia!' His mum's voice was stern.

'You are not to go near that place, do you hear me? That guy may be crazy, or may just hate kids.'

Tommy nodded. But as they headed out of the door, he memorized the name of the shop. It was Soo Long Antiques.

Tommy wondered if the man had followed them from Hyde Park and allowed himself to be seen just to give Tommy the message that he had the fish. Maybe he didn't have it at all, and was just trying to get Tommy off track.

Well, he'd find it wasn't that easy. Carp who become dragons swim upstream, Tommy reminded himself. If Wright could do it, he could do it.

Remembering what to say to whom was getting complicated: Calder and Petra knew one part of the story, and his mum knew another. He wasn't sure how much Ms Hussey or Mr Dare knew. And Goldman, witness and listener, probably knew the most.

Goldman would help him navigate.

The temperature rose that evening. By the time Tommy turned out his light, it was over thirty-two degrees. He insisted that he keep Goldman and his bed by the window, so his mum bought and installed hardware-store blinds that night.

'I don't care how hot it is or what my fortune cookie told me,' she said. 'I won't have anyone in that spooky old place looking in our windows.'

As soon as his mum had said good night, Tommy gently pulled up his blind. Propped on his elbows, he peered out at the Robie House.

Talk to me, he said silently to the house. *Tell me who has the fish. If only you could talk.*

A lone seagull cawed overhead. Two people walked by on Woodlawn Avenue, their heels clicking cheerfully on the pavement. The moon came out from behind a cloud, and light flashed and glimmered on Wright's magical glass. At night the triangles always seemed to stand out, and Tommy wondered what kind of a code Wright could possibly have left behind. Certainly not the Wright Sandwich Code, he smiled to himself. If only he and Calder and Petra could get inside to look.

Just then he saw something moving in the shadows on the side of the house. A dog? He peered around the side of Goldman's bowl to get a better look.

He saw two figures dressed in dark clothing. Tommy could now hear whispering. They crouched in the bushes, out of sight of the street, until it was absolutely quiet: no cars coming, no sounds of people. Then one of them pulled a ladder out from where they were hiding and placed it expertly, at just the right height, under a second-floor window.

Moving Goldman's bowl gently to one side, Tommy knocked two batteries off his window sill and they fell to the bare floor with a nasty metallic clatter. The figures stopped moving and looked towards his building.

Not knowing how much they could see, Tommy ducked back on his bed. A moment later a torchbeam combed his window screen, pausing momentarily on Goldman's bowl. He realized then that the water in the bowl was still sloshing.

'Stay still!' he whispered to Goldman.

He counted to fifty. Cautiously, he peered out again. The ladder was back on the ground, and the figures had vanished. Were they in the house?

Stretching out on his stomach with his chin on the window sill, he watched and waited. He could hear faint sounds of clinking and scraping, but he saw no lights through the dark windows.

What had his Moon Palace fortune said? Something about not giving up, and working in the dark. His heart pounding, he slipped out of bed and reached for shorts and a T-shirt. His mum's breathing was deep and even – she wouldn't wake up.

The new lock on the front door was silent, and Tommy eased it open ever so slowly. Under the light of a red emergency bulb, he padded down the stairs in bare feet. Outside the front door the air felt sweet and full, and the street was frighteningly quiet.

Creeping around the corner of his apartment building, he stayed as close to the ground as possible. When he was under his own window, he lay down in a flower bed and waited.

No one walked by, and time was marked only by distant sirens and the occasional movement of a cloud in front of the moon. The earth felt deliciously cool beneath his belly, and he was just starting to feel sleepy and relaxed when a sharp sparkle of light, zipping sideways across the Wright windows, caught one of the segments of glass. A triangle of gold floated above the flat surface. Almost instantly, it was gone.

Could that be a torch, a person moving around inside the house?

Then the window on the second floor, the one that had had the ladder beneath it, opened slowly. Tommy heard a low whistle and propped himself up on his elbows, straining to see in the dark.

Suddenly a heavy hand clapped him on the shoulder, and when he gasped, recoiling from the touch, a powerful flash went off in his face, not once but twice.

For several seconds, he was blinded.

He heard steps running, but by the time his vision was clear there was no one in sight. His heart pounded so wildly he felt sure everyone in the world could hear it. Looking up at the Robie House to see if it was safe to turn his back and race home, Tommy had the distinct feeling that the building was watching him, peering kindly through the darkness to see if he was hurt.

Once upstairs, with the door safely locked and his damp clothes bundled into a corner, Tommy looked out. The second-floor window was closed now and the house still.

Blinded by a flash ... That was something that had happened in Hitchcock's movie *Rear Window*. Only in that movie, the person with the flash had been the good guy.

Who had taken his picture, and what were they going to do with it?

Chapter Twenty-eight

THE JAPANESE GARDEN

The next morning was bright and clear. As Tommy's mum buttered toast and poured orange juice, she said lightly, 'I can't believe it's the fifteenth of June. We've only been back for two weeks and a day, and so much has happened.'

'Yup,' Tommy said. He glanced at the fish bowl. It was a good thing Goldman kept secrets.

'I'll be home early,' his mum said. 'And I want to enrol you in that sports camp on the mornings that I work. But for the rest of this week ... don't go anywhere in the neighbourhood without a friend. Are any other kids around?'

'Sure,' Tommy said. 'I'll phone Calder.'

'Well, don't forget what I said last night. Be extra careful. There are lots of Wright houses, but I only have one son.' His mum smiled at him, but Tommy could see a crease of worry under her blue eye.

As soon as his mum closed and locked the door, Tommy picked up the phone. 'Want to go to the Japanese Garden for our meeting?'

'Sure,' Calder said.

'I have an idea, but we need space to try it out.'

'Great. We'll be over in ten minutes.'

The Wright Three headed under the 59th Street overpass and towards the back of the Museum of Science and Industry. Once behind the museum, they followed a cracked pavement towards a narrow bridge. Since Tommy had told them he wanted to talk when they reached the garden, the three were quiet.

Wooded Island was in the middle of a lagoon. Over the decades it had become a sanctuary for white herons, families of ducks, songbirds of all kinds, a few beavers, old turtles and quiet Hyde Parkers. On the south-east end of the island sat the small but jewel-like Japanese Garden.

Stepping inside its high wooden gates, the Wright Three came to a complete stop.

'It's so magical,' Petra said.

The boys nodded.

Narrow paths of red pebbles ribboned to right and left around a small pool and towards the edge of the bigger lagoon. Bonsai trees, bushes with tiny, bell-like blossoms, a miniature weeping willow, and cropped, emerald grass linked the two bodies of water. A scattering of stone lanterns and sit-here rocks surrounded the inner pool, which was fed by a waterfall.

Single file, the three walked forward. The path they chose led them to a line of flat stepping stones that in turn led to a small, steeply arched bridge that crossed the channel between pool and lagoon.

'It's just like the bridge Goldman has now,' Tommy said. 'My mum and I bought it yesterday.'

'Where did you find the jade fish, Tommy?' Calder asked.

A cloud crossed Tommy's face, and he spun around quickly, as if orienting himself, then pointed to an area under some bushes. The three walked over. The dirt beneath looked hard-packed.

'I covered it up well,' he muttered.

'You sure this was where?' Calder asked. There

was an edge to his voice.

'Sure!' Tommy barked back. 'You don't believe me?'

'I do,' Calder said, but he didn't sound convinced.

Petra was standing on a heart-shaped rock. 'Look – there's a miniature island inside this pool that's just like a fish flipping its tail in the air! I never noticed it before.'

'Cool,' Tommy agreed. 'Hey, you guys want to see what I brought and hear my idea?' The three went over to the waterfall, where they could sit and dangle bare feet in the water while they talked. Tommy told them about the night before – the guy with the black glasses in Chinatown, the two figures in the bushes, the ladder and the blinding flash. Their eyes were huge, and Tommy sat back with satisfaction.

'Brave,' Petra murmured.

'Lucky,' Calder said.

'Why didn't you wake your mum up and call the police?' Petra asked.

Tommy shrugged. 'I guess I didn't want to worry her, and ... I thought maybe we three could do a better job than the police.'

'These guys could have the fish – who knows?' Tommy finished. 'We might get a clue to their plans.'

'And when we're in the house, we can take a look around,' Calder said, rattling his pentominoes happily. 'I believe the story about Wright leaving some kind of code, and if we can find it we might get enough publicity to save the house, even without the fish.'

'But how will we get in?' Petra sounded less enthusiastic.

'Simple: same way those guys did.' Tommy smiled. 'Because of the work on the house, that ladder is always on the side. And last night they didn't turn up until late, after midnight. We'll be there early, as soon as it's dark.'

'How about parents?' Calder asked.

'Thought of that too,' Tommy said proudly. 'We can ask to go to a nine o'clock movie at Delia Dell Hall, just a couple of blocks away from my place. The movie tomorrow night is *The Three Musketeers*. They won't mind us seeing that. My mum can walk us over there and then pick us up. She'll never know we weren't there in between.'

Petra clapped her hands. 'Brilliant!' she said. 'Kind of scary, but ... at least there'll be three of us.' Then Petra told them about the voice that had got into her head yesterday, and what it had said. She also told them about the *superstitious inklings* passage in *The Invisible Man*.

They spent the next half-hour spread out around the garden, testing the baby monitor. With new batteries, they could hear each other whisper at fifteen metres – their system should work easily between Tommy's apartment and the Robie House.

As they stood up to go, Tommy passed the red herring bag. Everybody ate one. Then Petra said, 'Sorry I called you despicable yesterday, Tommy. I was upset.'

'Sorry I lied to you guys,' Tommy mumbled, looking down at the pond. Just then a huge orange carp swished through the water centimetres from the base of the waterfall, its bright fins undulating in the dark water.

'Maybe that's a sign,' Petra said. 'The carp is telling us not to give up.'

'Right,' Tommy said.

As they left the garden, Tommy looked back at the lagoon and thought he saw the tiny island, the one shaped like a fish, lift its tail ever so slightly.

Chapter Twenty-nine

INSIDE AT NIGHT

As Calder, Petra and Tommy set off the next night for the movies, fireflies dotted the Robie House lawn and garden, and the sky above the Wright building glowed a dusky blue.

Tommy's mum stood on the corner and watched until they were out of sight. After all, as Tommy had pointed out, it seemed silly for her to walk them right to the door of the cinema when it was still light outside. The three had agreed not to look towards the Robie House, and they marched along in a stiff line, hardly noticing the summer evening.

They circled around the block and crept up the alleyway behind the house. Moving one by one, they hid in the bushes between a weathered tool shed and a pile of lumber.

Within half an hour it was dark. Waiting until they couldn't hear any traffic or pedestrian noises, the three crept out of their hiding place.

While Calder and Petra crouched in the shadows

next to the Robie House, Tommy ran out to the pavement and peered both ways. He gave a thumbs-up sign. While the other two manoeuvred the ladder up against the building, Tommy dashed back, the three made sure it was steady, and he started to climb.

Calder and Petra watched anxiously from below. When he reached the window, Tommy gave the glass a gentle push. Nothing. He pushed again. Still nothing.

'It's locked!' he whispered, and leaned out from the ladder and squinted along the second floor. To his left he saw a window that didn't meet the sill in the same spot as the others.

He hurried down, and the three hustled the ladder several metres along the building and repeated the whole procedure. As Tommy climbed the second time, they heard feet coming down the street. It was too late to hide, and the kids froze.

The feet moved on past the house, and Calder and Petra gave each other a silent high-five: so far, so good.

Tommy was outside the second window now

and pushed gently. It creaked open, swinging inward about fifteen centimetres, and stopped with a dull thunk. Tommy reached his hand cautiously inside. He felt around for several seconds and carefully pulled the window shut again, holding on to the leading in the glass with his fingers.

Petra was secretly glad it wasn't her hand reaching into the blackness.

'There's something like a file cabinet inside,' Tommy whispered as he climbed back down.

'Let's keep trying,' Calder whispered back and, after leaving the ladder just where they had found it, they crept along the east wall of the Robie House property, by the garage, and ducked inside the gates. Slipping through an opening that led to the south side of the house, they found themselves in the garden next to the first-floor terrace.

Just then they heard voices, and sank to a sitting position with their backs to the garden wall. This side of the house was brighter than the rear because of street lights, and it would be more difficult not to be seen.

The walking stopped on the other side of the

wall, and they heard the jingle of metal tags and the pant-snuffle-snuffle of a large dog.

'Imagine the second-floor windows at night! I understand it looked wonderful, all those round lamps lit like so many moons ...' Next they heard a plastic bag scrunching.

'Yes, so sad about the house coming down,' the second voice said, muffled by bending over to pick up something.

The three kids smelled the something. After the dog walkers had gone, Tommy unpinched his nose. 'I'm glad I have a goldfish!'

Petra giggled.

'Shh ... more people,' Calder whispered.

As they waited in silence for them to go by, Petra gazed at the first-floor windows, once the children's playroom, and thought of Fred Robie's son in his little car, zooming in and out of the door to the courtyard, imagining nothing but a blissful present. Suddenly she felt pulled by the passage of time as if by a dark current, and wondered if one day some unknown person would think of her, a young girl with puffy hair and glasses, sitting in this garden on a summer night.

'Someone told me there are ghosts in here.' The voice was young, and sounded a little like Ms Hussey.

'Yeah, like the ghosts in your library study room,' someone else said. 'You'd better get to work on that project and stop messing around.'

'And you should mind your own business,' the first voice said as they moved out of earshot.

'I like being invisible,' Petra whispered.

The three sat silently for several more minutes. Calder looked over at the front terrace, to their left, and Tommy stared up at the second-floor balcony.

'I could probably get in those French doors,' he whispered.

'Come on!' Calder said.

They crept, single file, up the steps to the terrace. Up three, around a corner, up eight more ... Suddenly Calder felt as if he were climbing a giant W, turning right by a T, passing an L. He was moving into a dark pentomino world, a world of concrete and brick, a world made up of massive pieces he could no longer control. It's a trick of the

shadows, he told himself firmly. It doesn't feel threatening during the day. Pay attention to what you're doing.

A short wall next to them was the same height as the wall around the second-floor balcony, but a gap yawned between the parapets, a gap that opened over the cement walkway below. The drop was at least four metres.

Tommy climbed up on the wall. 'It's too far to jump with such a narrow place to land.'

'How about using some of that wood by the tool shed?' Calder said.

Minutes later, they had a plank about thirty centimetres wide and three metres long up on the terrace. They laid it flat between the two walls, bridging the gap between terrace and balcony.

'Not good,' Petra said. 'That would be a wicked fall.'

'Let's try the roof,' Calder suggested. 'If one of us gets up, maybe we can open a bedroom window.'

After a three-way conference about weight and height, Tommy and Petra made a square platform out of their arms by gripping each other's wrists.

Calder stepped up on it, one hand on each head. Straightening centimetre by centimetre, hardly breathing, he reached over his head and grabbed the copper drain at the edge of the roof.

'Got it,' he whispered, and began to pull himself up. An ominous, scratchy groan was followed by a metallic twang and a jolt. Calder looked down for the first time, and the ground far below lurched up at a sickening angle.

'Yeow!' he gasped as he let go. The three collapsed in a painful heap on the concrete terrace. Tommy had spiked Petra in the ribs, and she found herself lying on someone's knee. They heard voices coming again and, hidden by the terrace wall, they untangled themselves silently. All were grateful for the dark.

'Isn't that a board up there between the two sections of terrace? Should we look?' a woman asked.

'Oh, you remember they're planning that pull-down,' a man replied. 'There's probably all kinds of bits of wood lying around.' The voices drifted on down the block.

'Sorry,' Calder sighed. 'At least the whole drain didn't come down.'

'Not your fault,' Tommy said.

'Maybe we should give up,' Petra said. 'It's already nine thirty.'

It was Tommy who hopped up on the wall of the terrace. Before the other two could say a word, he took a quick step on to the board and ran lightly across it, jumping to the balcony floor outside the French doors.

'Whoa!' Calder and Petra breathed in one startled voice.

'Throw me my backpack!' Tommy whispered. Calder did, and when he caught it there was a loud clunk-rattle-rattle. Calder worried, in a flash, that Tommy was too impulsive. Whoever had broken into the Robie House earlier would surely not mind doing something bad to a kid, especially a lone kid carrying a listening device.

Watching Tommy slip through the shadows, Petra felt her stomach tighten into an anxious knot. Had they meant to do something this dangerous? Tommy's round head looked vulnerable and small in the darkness. What had they been thinking, breaking into a wreck of a place that criminals had been in two nights before?

Tiptoeing along, Tommy tried every door handle. When he reached the end of the terrace, he stopped.

He knelt, and Calder and Petra watched him take off his trainer.

'Careful!' Calder whispered, but Tommy didn't seem to hear.

He pushed the heel of his shoe gently against one of the doors, just below the handle. He pushed harder, and his trainer shot out of sight.

'Must be a patched place in the glass,' Petra whispered to Calder.

As Tommy reached his hand slowly into the dark room, both Calder and Petra tried not to imagine someone inside grabbing him. After a series of rattles and creaks, the French door swung open. Tommy stumbled, made an odd choking sound, and disappeared inside.

'Was he *pulled*?' Petra gasped. She could picture him being dragged across the floor, a big hand clamped over his mouth.

'Let's knock on the windows in the prow,' Calder said anxiously. 'If he doesn't come, we'll start yelling.'

Chapter Thirty

THE NET

Tommy never forgot the feeling of first stepping into that house.

The living room was empty and the ceilings low. Black and white triangles and parallelograms spanned the windows on all sides, and light from the street threw a crosshatching of shadows across the floor, as if a net had been dropped neatly underfoot. Without colour outside or in, the lines of leading between the glass became magnetic, almost powerful.

A fish in a net! Tommy thought to himself; I'm held in a net. But instead of feeling caught, he felt embraced, almost loved. It was the strangest feeling, and for several minutes he stood without moving. The house had a dry, old smell that reminded him of something long ago, of very tall people and dark furniture ... it must be a memory so early that he'd almost forgotten it. How odd, he thought, that this feels so like home.

Hearing a gentle tapping on the glass at the far end of the room, he hurried over to look for a window that

would open off the front terrace. Tommy found one in the prow, unlocked it, and after a quick check up and down the street Calder and Petra scrambled in.

'Isn't this the coolest?' Tommy said. 'I love it!'

'Thanks for forgetting about us,' Calder muttered.

Standing inside, Petra's imagination was already slipping back through all the families in the house. There were the Robie kids, and then the five boys who loved to run. There was the family with two girls. This was the last house one of the girls ever knew … and had she seen it at night too, and looked at the same things Petra was looking at?

The younger sister had lived on in the house as an only child, and Petra remembered pictures of her dressed as a Spanish dancer, an elf, a gnome with a peaked cap. In one image, she stood by the second-floor French doors in a simple dress, half of her body dissolving in a radiant light. Her expression in all of those pictures was wistful and more than a little ghostly.

'Haunting,' Petra said, walking in a slow circle.

Calder was examining a series of wooden ceiling panels that lined the living room, grilles made up of long parallel bars with cubes fitted between them at irregular intervals. 'It's like sheet music,' he mused. 'Wait: those cubes are in groups of three ... Could be some kind of code ...'

Tommy gave him a quick punch on the arm. 'Come on! We've gotta find a good place to hide this monitor.'

The three crept quickly through the entire house. They twisted and turned, discovering three sets of stairs, and found it was hard to keep track of where they had been or what direction they were facing when they looked out. Up then down, right then left: narrow halls opened out into spacious rooms which then flowed back into thin passageways. The moon was full, and the leading in Wright's windows etched patterns that bent across the children's faces and fell cleanly on bare walls and floors, the patterns changing from room to room.

'We're in the middle of a giant game of cat's cradle,' Petra marvelled.

'Let's hope no one's playing,' Calder muttered.

Tools and sawhorses lay here and there, and littered throughout the kitchen area on the second floor, at the rear of the house, were paper cups and fast-food wrappers. Looking outside, Tommy spotted his own bedroom window, and thought he saw the faint curve of Goldman's bowl.

'Good,' he said.

'Huh?' Calder said.

'All this trash must mean they meet here.' Tommy was already pulling the baby monitor out of his backpack.

Petra opened the door beneath the kitchen sink, and there was a sudden scrabble and a loud squeak. The three jumped, and Petra grabbed for the closest arm, which happened to be Tommy's. Recovering her balance, she let go quickly.

'How about on one of these shelves?' Tommy asked, stepping up on a milk crate. He placed the monitor carefully between a stack of paper plates and a nasty cheese grater.

'Fine,' Petra said, moving away from the sink.

'You're sure you turned it on?' Calder asked Tommy.

'Yup,' Tommy nodded happily, clicking on the hand-held receiver and fastening it to his belt.

Just then they heard a slow, irregular step in a distant part of the house. It was a person walking, but walking hesitantly. One, two ... The steps paused, as if someone were listening, and then started again. Three, four ... The Wright Three stared wildly at one another, hardly daring to breathe. A ghost? All the stories they'd ever heard about hauntings flashed and sizzled in their minds: pirates, thieves, murderers, miserable souls ...

Several seconds of complete silence felt like hours. Even the building itself seemed to be holding its breath. Five ... The steps sounded like they were on the third floor, far enough away so that the three could still escape.

'Let's go!' Tommy hissed, and they ran back out of the kitchen, into the dining room, and towards the unlocked window in the prow. Halfway across the living room they froze, Petra piling up against Calder, who ran into Tommy. A man in dark clothing stood on the terrace. He had picked up the board that Tommy had sprinted across, and was looking at the casement window, the one the kids had left unlocked.

The Wright Three were trapped.

Chapter Thirty-one

THREE LITTLE BIRDIES

Calder, Petra and Tommy backed up, watching the man as he reached for the edge of the window. He stopped and put the board down. In the second before he pulled the window open, the kids understood the craziness and danger of what they were doing. No parents knew where they were, and they hadn't left a note.

The three turned and raced back through the dining room towards the swing door to the kitchen. As they ran, a flashlight behind them went on and off, playing across their backs.

'Stick together!' Calder said. 'Three to one!'

For several endless seconds they pulled and yanked on the back-door knob, but the lock wouldn't give. All three paused, listening – there was no sound from the living room.

The man must know the back door wouldn't open. But where was he? Which way was he coming? A long hall connected the kitchen with the dining room and living room. They had just come through the pantry, which opened back into the dining room, forming a circle.

A board popped, loudly, from the direction of the dining room.

'Upstairs!' whispered Tommy.

Instinctively, the three then did something they would never have done under other circumstances – they grabbed for each other's hands, forming a human chain.

Just then the swing door to the pantry burst open and they took off, tearing through the dark channels of space that had seemed so magical just minutes earlier.

Two scary corners loomed ahead: one connected the kitchen passageway to the back hall, the other the hall to the third-floor stairwell. They rounded both without meeting anyone, and pounded up the stairs to the third floor. There wasn't time to worry about heading towards the ghostly steps they'd heard just moments before – heavy footsteps were gaining behind them.

A deep voice called out: 'It's three kids! Stop them!'

The moment they rushed into the first bedroom a heavy covering came down on their heads and rough arms squeezed them against the wall.

Calder punched and kicked, Tommy bit and Petra shrieked 'Ow!' as the footsteps thumped heavily into the room.

'You wanna get hurt? Just keep it up, I got no problem breaking a few arms,' a second voice growled.

The Wright Three stopped moving. The covering smelled nasty, and something was burning Calder's nose. Suddenly he sneezed, and then again.

'Eeuw,' Petra mouthed, wiping off her cheek.

The tarpaulin was pulled off. The kids found themselves facing two men with black net masks on their heads. One of them wore black glasses over the mask.

'A *girl*?'

'Looks like it,' Black Glasses said. He jabbed his finger at Tommy. 'Thought I told you to stay away from here. Wrecking your place not enough?'

'A murder is announced!' the other scoffed.

It was Petra who spoke first. 'We didn't mean anything – we're just kids from the neighbourhood.'

'Yeah, kids with enough nosiness to take us all down,' Black Glasses said.

As he spoke, he pulled a knife off his belt and ripped the tarpaulin into several long strips. He tied the kids' arms behind their backs, and then, pushing them into a back-to-back triangle, ran a long tight strip around all three of their waists. They squirmed miserably.

'There. You'll drive each other crazy before you get anywhere.'

'Looks like we'll have to speed up the whole plan,' Black Glasses said to the other man, who had a long, thin head.

'You mean fire it tonight?' Thin Head said.

'No choice. There are plenty of flammables we can use in the garage. Can't keep these three little birdies around.'

'I got four windows ready to go on the second floor. How many you got up here?'

'Two in the master. One across the hall.'

'That's enough to take us to the islands and find a dealer for the jade.'

So he did have the fish! Tommy nudged Calder, and Black Glasses noticed. He bent down until he was eye to eye with Tommy, their noses almost touching. Tommy froze.

'Thanks for the fish, kid. Sometimes you win, sometimes you lose,' the man said slowly.

As he turned away, Petra tried to stifle a sob.

'And don't even try the crying thing, girlie,' he snarled.

If there was one thing Petra hated, it was being criticized for being a girl. A tiny flame of anger began to sizzle inside her.

The three stood quietly as Black Glasses headed back downstairs. Thin Head picked up a hammer, and after snorting, 'Be good, kiddies. And keep your mouths shut,' he went across the hall. Tap-tap-tapping and the squeaking of wood came from below, and Tommy recognized the sounds he'd heard faintly last night.

Fired ... All three kids guessed this meant setting the house on fire. *Can't keep these three little birdies* ... Were they really planning to burn down the Robie House with three kids tied up inside?

If the kids hadn't been together that night, they might not have been able to be as strong, but as they stood there, hearts pounding and brains racing, all three reached the same angry conclusion: They wouldn't give up.

Petra had an idea.

'Sir? Is it OK if we pray?' she called to Thin Head.

There was an exaggerated sigh. 'Please yourself,' he barked back.

'N-T-N-R-N-Y-N L-E-L-S-L-C-L-A-L-P-L-E-L,' Petra said in a slow monotone. She emphasized every other letter in each word, hoping that if she only used one pentomino for the bread in the Wright Sandwich Code they could communicate aloud.

There was a short silence, and Thin Head called, 'Hey! That ain't English.'

'It's Romanian Latin. We learned it in school. It's called the Chant for Lost Children,' Petra called back, hoping Thin Head hadn't studied Latin and wasn't Eastern European.

Tommy said, 'I-R-I-O-I-O-I-F-I.'

Then Calder said, 'N-A-N-S-N-K-N V-T-V-O-V Z-P-Z-E-Z-E-Z.'

After figuring out what Calder had said, Petra cleared her throat. 'Sir? I have to use the bathroom. Bad.'

'Jeez!' the man bellowed, stomping into the room. 'He *would* leave me to babysit you, wouldn't he?'

Wisely, the three said nothing. As the man untied the strip around their waists, they stood meekly. Petra even ventured a grateful smile. The man untied her hands.

'Ours too?' Calder asked. 'Just while she's in there?'

'You try anything when I untie your hands, you'll be sorry,' he said to the boys. 'Understand? Face to the wall while she's using the toilet.'

The boys nodded, eyes on the floor.

'Don't lock the door!' the man ordered as Petra walked into the bathroom.

As soon as she sat down noisily on the toilet seat, trousers still on, there was a wild scuffling and grunting in the bedroom. She jumped up and ran back in. Thin Head was bent over double, clutching his middle. While Tommy frantically wrapped the man's head like a mummy with strips of fabric, Calder clung to his back in a fierce hug, bouncing and sliding as Thin Head tried to throw him off. Petra rushed over to help, adding her weight to Calder's, and Thin Head stumbled to his knees. Tommy tied a quick knot and hopped to one side.

Calder let go and jerked open one of the casement windows. Petra, staggering backward, lost her balance and hit the wall. Thin Head was now back on his feet and pulling at the fabric on his eyes and mouth. At the sound of the thump, a groping arm lunged in Petra's direction. Tommy stomped his foot, and Thin Head swung the other way.

Calder slipped through the window, reached back for Petra's hand, and pulled as hard as he could. She shot through, landing on her knees, and Tommy followed. They scrambled over metal flower boxes and dropped on to the roof above the living room.

A wild, angry shouting came from inside the house, and Thin Head's body squeezed out of the window after them, his black net mask now sitting on his head like a crooked sock hat.

'Punks!' he choked. 'Little creeps!'

Black Glasses, who had had been out in the garage during the scuffle, heard the kids landing on the roof. He ran to the front terrace and looked up from below.

'Come on down, kids!' he called softly. 'I'll catch you!'

Calder, Petra and Tommy hurried to the end of the farthest ridge, their feet sliding on the rounded tile. They couldn't go any further without falling.

'Help!' Petra's voice came out in a squeak.

'Help!' Tommy and Calder echoed, but they didn't see anyone in the street. No cars drove by.

Now just steps away, Thin Head walked towards them in a half-crouch, arms wide. Sweat glistened on his face and neck.

'Got you,' he snarled.

Clinging to each other, the Wright Three sank into a terrified heap. Tears ran silently down Petra's face and Calder's teeth chattered uncontrollably. One of Tommy's knees trembled so violently that it thumped up and down against the hard tile, beating a weird rhythm in the dark.

Could they survive a push? Should they let go of each other? How had they ended up on a slippery roof, in the middle of the night, with an angry criminal?

Petra thought of her family and of never seeing her words in print; Calder thought of his parents and of all the problem-solving he hadn't yet done; Tommy thought of his mum and Goldman.

And then something very odd happened. Either Thin Head's knees buckled beneath him, making the roof look as though it rose in a wave, or the roof itself heaved upward. None of the three were ever quite sure what they had seen.

Thin Head was suddenly airborne, his mouth open, his arms bent like stiff wings. He hit the roof on his side and rolled over and over down the north slope, clutching desperately at the tile. Every piece he grabbed pulled loose in his hand. He bounced across the gutter and vanished into darkness, accompanied by the crack-shatter of terracotta hitting the cement walk below.

A heavy grunt was followed by silence.

'What the—' Black Glasses exclaimed. Heavy footsteps ran to see what had happened, and the kids heard a terrible screeching sound and the clang of falling metal. A cloud of debris and dust rose from the terrace. Again, there was silence.

Slowly, ever so slowly, the Wright Three let go of each other. No words came at first. Needing to know if they were safe or whether the men were coming after them again, they inched carefully along the ridge, glancing back at the open window and the dark house behind. Finally they spotted Thin Head lying on the walkway on the north side. Nearby, one of Black Glasses' legs stuck out from beneath a pile of plaster and bent copper.

'Oh!' Petra breathed, half laughing, half crying. 'We made it!'

'Safe!' Tommy whispered.

'Alive,' Calder gasped.

'Did you *see* that?' Tommy asked in a shaky voice.

'I can't believe it,' Calder croaked. 'I really can't.'

'What happened?' Petra asked. 'How come we're OK?'

Tommy tugged on the tile around him, but nothing gave. Calder lifted his shoulders in a long, happy shrug.

'Either we're incredibly, insanely lucky, or ...' Petra's voice trailed off.

The other two nodded.

Petra reached down and patted the roof gently. 'Thank you, house,' she whispered. She kissed one hand and touched it to the tile.

A breeze rippled through the trees, and a wash of light danced across the third-floor windows, pausing at the casement where the kids had escaped. As they watched, the window swung slowly closed and the boiled-sweet shape in the centre gleamed.

Chapter Thirty-two

LOST AND FOUND

The three kids were rescued from the roof in a fire engine bucket and parents were called. Tommy's mum had been having a late dinner with friends near the campus, and was reached on her mobile phone. Calder's and Petra's parents were at a party several blocks away, but were coming. Dazed, the Wright Three sat in a line on the pavement.

Tommy dropped his head into his hands and covered his eyes.

'What?' Calder asked.

Tommy said abruptly, 'Gotta tell.'

'What?' Calder asked again.

'I *did* find the fish here. I lied about the Japanese Garden. I was just so confused about what to do.'

'You lied to us about lying?' Petra asked, looking at Tommy as if he were from another planet.

'Why?' Calder asked.

'I thought I had to,' Tommy said. 'But now Black Glasses has the fish. Everything will be out in the

open, and I'll feel bad if everyone thinks I'm some kind of hero. Since I trespassed and found it on this property, it probably belongs to the university anyway. Now they can sell it, just like you said. If I told everyone I found it in the Japanese Garden, and then we tried to sell it for the Robie House, the Chicago Parks Department might take it and who knows what would happen then.' Tommy glanced at Petra and chewed his thumbnail.

Petra, to his relief, didn't get angry. 'That's pretty good thinking.'

Tommy shrugged. 'Finders have to think that way.' He paused and cleared his throat. 'And the Wright Three matters a whole lot to me.'

Petra looked at him, her head on one side. 'Me too,' she said.

Calder nodded. He didn't think he'd ever heard Tommy say as much about how he felt.

The three were silent for a moment.

'That fish has been lost and found a lot,' Petra murmured. 'First Wright bought it, then he lost it ... then you found it, then you lost it ... Black Glasses found it and is about to lose it ... and now it's coming back to Wright.'

'Yeah,' Tommy said slowly. 'Maybe sometimes when you lose something, you end up getting something else. Only you can't know about the second thing until you've lost the first.'

'I like that,' Petra said. 'Like losing is sometimes gaining. I'll have to think about that.'

'Sure,' Tommy said, sucking in his cheeks.

All five of the Wright Three parents were horrified when they found out what their children had been up to, and after the hugs there were several hours of lectures and angry exclamations that night. But the adults couldn't stay upset for long – after all, their kids had saved a great home and a great work of art, something only Frank Lloyd Wright had been able to do before them.

The Wright Three were relieved to hear that Black Glasses and Thin Head were going to make it. As soon as they had recovered enough to talk, they were put under arrest and the pieces of the story fell into place.

The men were brothers. Petty criminals who had

always worked for a boss, they heard about the Robie House plans from an informer in New York. Being unemployed at the time, they decided to apply to the crew on their own, planning to pocket what they could on the job – lamps were what they had in mind. They faked two sets of credentials, and were hired.

On their first day in the house, on 1st June, they heard the story of the jade talisman from Henry Dare. The young man was proud to be the great-grandson of the mason who had built the house with Wright. He wanted to be an expert, and was happy to share his family secret. After all, the house was coming down, and the fish was long gone.

As the crew worked on plans for partitioning the house, they were told by the foreman about the tremendous value of the windows, and about the hazards of Wright's wiring. Many of his houses, after all, had burned to the ground. They were warned to work slowly and carefully.

A new idea, a very greedy idea, began to form in the minds of the brothers. Their plan would be easy to execute: sneak in at night, gradually loosen a few windows, and escape with their plunder as the house went up in flames. Because of the fire, no one would know which windows had been stolen. Now working for themselves, Black Glasses and Thin Head had connections, and planned to sell the Wright windows for a fortune.

They hadn't counted on the Wright Three showing up. The brothers swore they wouldn't have left Tommy, Petra and Calder in a burning house, but the kids weren't so sure. *Can't keep these three little birdies* ... Those words weren't easy to forget.

On the afternoon of 3rd June, the day Ms Hussey read the article to her class and the day Henry Dare fell, Black Glasses pretended to have left his wristwatch inside, and went back into the Robie House by himself as the crew drove away. The foreman, who was late for a dentist appointment, had let him in and instructed him to close the front door firmly when he left. In reality, Black Glasses was going back in to open the latch on a kitchen window so that he and his brother could return after dark.

Looking out of a first-floor window, Black

Glasses saw a boy dash across the south-side garden. He watched as the kid knelt down and dug furiously for several minutes, and then hopped up with a small object in his hand.

The kid was obviously excited, and ran into the apartment building next door. As Black Glasses stood puzzling over what he had just seen, he remembered the mason's story about Wright's lost talisman.

⊞ ⊞ ⊞ Once out of the hospital, Henry Dare saw the sixth-grade demonstration on 9th June and talked with Ms Hussey. He had quit the crew by then, and wanted to help save the Robie House. But besides that ... well, the teacher was pretty interesting.

When he asked her out on a date, she suggested a trip to the Art Institute. The moment Mr Dare saw the Asian wing, he thought of Frank Lloyd Wright's talisman story. He decided to take Ms Hussey on a mini treasure hunt in the museum. He liked surprises himself, and was curious about what they might find. Besides that, he wanted to impress her.

⊞ ⊞ ⊞ Black Glasses saw Tommy leave the

apartment that morning. While he couldn't watch the building every second, he knew Tommy often peered out of his window, and the boy's blind had been still for over an hour. Black Glasses asked his brother to cover for him. He crept over to Tommy's apartment, listened at the door and broke in.

It didn't take long to find the carving. When Black Glasses brought it to Chinatown that evening to ask about its value, he was stunned by what he learned. The brothers would live like kings once they'd found the right collector to buy it.

That night, the two of them came back to the Robie House to continue their work on the windows. It was Thin Head who found Tommy outside in the flower bed and blinded him with a camera flash, something he always carried for just such an emergency.

The following night Thin Head had been waiting for his brother and taking a nap on the third floor when the Wright Three broke into the house. He said he was asleep under a tarpaulin when he heard the kids running downstairs, so the steps that Calder, Petra and Tommy had heard moments earlier were not his.

Black Glasses and Thin Head were tried for attempted burglary, assault and wilful destruction of private property, and both went to prison.

田田田 When John Stone, the President of the University of Chicago, heard what the Wright Three had done to save the house, he was more than impressed. He was moved.

Black Glasses had the jade fish in his pocket when he was pulled from under the debris on the night of 16th June. Tommy explained to President Stone that he'd found the fish in the Robie House garden, and he hoped it could be sold to help with the renovation. Calder, Petra and Tommy suggested that the university take it to the Art Institute for an evaluation. They did, and it was found to be worth a great deal of money.

The university set up the Wright Fund, and began plans for a massive renovation. When the press heard that the house had been saved by three children who had not only risked their lives but also found a real treasure and donated it to the cause, the money poured in. The house got more attention than it had since Wright had last saved it himself, almost fifty years before.

President Stone announced that they would open the house to the public during restoration, in order to build up more funds and support, and that the university would create a small gift shop and a caretaker's apartment on the site. The gift shop would have Wright books and cards, and the job of running it would come with a small salary but the added compensation of the apartment.

When Zelda Segovia applied for the job, the President was thrilled to discover that Tommy, his mum and Goldman wanted to live in the house. He promised them the north-east side of the second floor – a giant kitchen, two small bedrooms and their own entrance. And he said it was fine, once the house was finished, if they used the rest of it when it was closed to the public.

Zelda Segovia dreamed of morning tea on a terrace, and Tommy couldn't wait to be the first kid to live in the house since 1926. Goldman kept an eye on the restoration and waited patiently for the view from his own Wright window.

Chapter Thirty-three

HE'S HERE!

Once the first excitement had died down, the Wright Three agreed that they had unfinished business: the part of himself that Wright coded into the Robie House hadn't been found.

After explaining their mission, the children asked President Stone if they could visit the house during the day. They wanted to invite Ms Hussey, Mrs Sharpe and Mr Dare. The President had heard Mr Dare's story about Wright's code, and he agreed. Everyone was curious.

⊞⊞⊞ On the morning of 21st June, the President unlocked the front door of the Robie House and they all stepped inside. Mr Dare pointed out some of his great-grandfather's work on the fireplaces, and Ms Hussey marvelled at the poetry of Wright's windows. President Stone admired everything, and Mrs Sharpe stomped around with her cane.

In daylight, the colours of the art glass – cream, amber, sepia – traced delicate, plant-like forms on the streetscape outside. The kids hadn't realized Wright's ingenious plan for privacy: from the inside the colours were muted, but from the outside, they shimmered like polished abalone, making it difficult to look in. The net they had seen at night shifted to a lacy screen during the day.

Tommy circled around, practically hugging himself, humming happily.

Petra stood in the middle of the living room. She waited until the grown-ups were all in the dining room, and said to Calder and Tommy, 'I brought one of my copies of *The Invisible Man*. I'm going to ask it for help in looking for the code.'

Just days ago, Tommy would have teased her about doing this, but he only said, 'Cool.'

She pulled a copy of the book out of her back pocket, closed her eyes, and leafed back and forth through it. Pointing to the middle of a page, she opened her eyes and read:

If a man were made of glass, he would still be visible ...

The Wright Three looked at each other. 'The only glass is in the windows,' Petra said.

Mrs Sharpe's bony face peeked around the fireplace, her green eyes bright. 'That's correct. Remember when I said you have everything you need?'

'Yes,' Petra said slowly. 'So if a man were made of glass, he couldn't be the Invisible Man. But you said *sometimes visible, sometimes not* ... Hmm.'

Calder frowned. 'I've thought of the windows already. I counted geometric shapes and tried to sort them into an alphabet, but it doesn't work. There's nothing there.'

'How about if we just look for a man-shape in one of the windows?' Tommy asked.

Mrs Sharpe sat down next to the hearth.

'But do you know where the code is?' Petra asked her.

The old woman looked vague and patted her bun. 'Memory is a tricky thing,' she said slowly.

'Want to come upstairs with us?' Ms Hussey called from the foot of the third-floor stairwell.

'Still looking down here,' Petra called back. The

kids split up and walked slowly around the dining room and living room. Mrs Sharpe didn't move.

'Hey!' Tommy stopped in front of a slender casement window tucked into the prow at the north end of the living room. The window was one of a pair, the panels symmetrically folded into the V-shaped wall in a way that made them almost invisible.

'Look!' Tommy's voice was now bright and eager. 'I think it's a man, like a man a kid might draw!'

Calder and Petra rushed over.

'See? A head – with two eyes and a nose.'

'And arms bent at the elbows,' Petra added. '*Three* sets of arms, like the Buddha-woman in the Asian wing!'

'And long legs, and little triangle feet,' Calder exclaimed. He whacked his old friend on the back, and Petra gave him a wild high-five.

Mrs Sharpe got to her feet. 'Bravo,' she said.

The Wright Three beamed.

'We found him!' Tommy shouted. 'Come and see! It's Frank Lloyd Wright!'

While Mr Stone, Ms Hussey and Mr Dare hurried downstairs, Calder stood in front of the man and stirred his pentominoes. He pulled the I out of his pocket, and held it against the glass as if it were a short ruler. Moving it back and forth across the window, he counted under his breath.

He spun around and whooped.

'It's a Fibonacci man!' Calder crowed.

As everyone watched, Calder measured the width of the hat on top of the head.

'That's unit one,' he said.

Then he measured the width of the face. 'Two.'

Then he measured the collar. 'Three.'

Then he measured the widest set of arms. 'Five.'

He counted thirteen parallelograms running in a strip down both sides of the body. 'Wright coded himself in Fibonacci numbers!' he marvelled.

'And it took us thirteen days to save the house,' Petra said. 'And we're turning thirteen this year.'

'And we're the Wright Three,' Tommy added.

'And today is the twenty-first. I'll bet there are tons of other Fibonacci numbers if we go back and look,' Calder said. 'Weird – just like all this is a part of some big design.'

The group was silent for a moment, everyone's minds fizzing with ideas.

'I knew about the glass man years ago, and was somehow never surprised,' Mrs Sharpe said. 'After all, this was a house built for children. But the Fibonacci numbers ... very intriguing, I must say.'

Calder scratched his head happily with the I pentomino.

The President's mobile phone rang, echoing through the empty house.

'Excuse me,' he muttered turning away to take the call.

The President printed several words neatly in a small notebook he pulled out of his pocket. 'Yes, absolutely, so exciting! I'll tell them.'

Dropping the phone back in his pocket, he beamed at the group. 'What timing! That was an archivist who has been looking through Wright papers from the year 1905 for a reference to the jade fish. We're trying to verify its authenticity before selling it, as that of course will make it more valuable. He told me he found this entry, written on Japanese hotel stationery with a drafting pencil:

Bought small jade fish today. Will keep.

Stepping out of the Robie House minutes later, the President said goodbye and hurried back towards his campus office. The others stood outside and squinted into the morning light. A sparrow hopped along the terrace wall, sun sparkled on the Wright windows, and the fan-like leaves of a gingko tree spun first one way and then the other in the June breeze.

'That's incredible news about the 1905 note,' Ms Hussey said. 'What a coincidence that it came just as we found Wright's code!'

'I wonder what it is about coincidence and us,' Petra said. 'Does this happen to other people?'

When Mrs Sharpe spoke, her voice was uncharacteristically light. 'I don't think it's that unusual. I think most people don't know what to do with it, so they pay no attention. Coincidence reminds me of the repetitions of geometric pattern in the Robie House. The more you look, the more you see.'

Ms Hussey nodded. 'Maybe coincidence is just a tricky echo in the structure of people's lives, like the tricky echoes in shape and scale that Wright set up.'

'I like that,' Calder agreed.

'Echoes that tell you something,' Petra added.

Tommy grinned as he pulled a tired-looking sandwich bag out of his pocket. 'Who wants a red herring?' he asked.

Chapter Thirty-four

SUMMER IN HYDE PARK

By the end of the summer, Wright's jade fish had been bought by the Art Institute, who also bought the note on hotel stationery. Fish and note got their own display case in the Asian wing.

Interestingly enough, there were no further unexplained disturbances in the Robie House during the months of renovation – no more slamming doors, silvery voices or treacherous windows. No workers were hurt.

Calder, Petra and Tommy continued to meet regularly in the Castigliones' tree house. Calder spent most of the summer happily cutting long pieces of wood into perfect cubes, and making multiple sets of three-dimensional pentominoes. When he had thirteen sets, he built his own version of the Robie House.

Petra began her first book. The main character

was a girl, one who was 'sometimes visible and sometimes not', and had two close friends who were boys.

Calder and Petra often went with Tommy on scavenging expeditions; there were lots of places to dig in Hyde Park. His mum gave him a lovely stone fish, an old one from South America, and he began his collection over again. She also gave him a compass and a notebook for mapping each find.

After every rain that summer, the bare footprints of a man were spotted here and there in the mud that collected along the edges of gardens and pavements. No one thought much about it. But then, it was Hyde Park, the streets were empty and almost anything was possible.

AUTHOR'S NOTE

THE WRIGHT STORY

I read many books about Frank Lloyd Wright's life and work before I started to write, and I tried to follow the facts as closely as possible. However, I added or changed a few things. Here they are:

1. While the history of the Robie House is accurate, including the two near-demolitions in 1941 and 1957, the building is not currently in danger. It is now a National Historic Landmark, and is being taken care of by the Frank Lloyd Wright Preservation Trust, the University of Chicago, and the National Trust for Historic Preservation. Several million dollars have gone toward renovating the outside of the building, and renovation of the interior is still under way. It is open to the public during the day.

The planned fate of the Robie House in this book is close to what has happened to a number of famous and beautiful buildings. Hundreds of Wright windows and several rooms are currently in museums. Sad but true, works of art that large and fragile are difficult to save in one piece.

2. The story of the fish jumped into my mind as I got to know Mr Wright, and it seemed like it might have happened. Perhaps it did ... Over the years, he brought back many treasures from Japan, and he was both a dreamer and a man of huge ambition. The Asian legends in the story are real, and the fish itself exists. I 'borrowed' it for *The Wright Three* from the collection of the Smithsonian Institution's Arthur M. Sackler Gallery in Washington, D.C.

3. The man in the window is right where he has been since 1910, and can be seen at all times of day and in any season. He appears in

many photographs and reproductions of the Robie House.

Mr Wright wrote very little about the meaning of his art-glass window designs, and nothing about the existence of the man. Perhaps this shouldn't be surprising – Wright understood the magic of discovery, and never gave away his best secrets. ⊞ ⊞ ⊞